T0365580

A Perfect Fit

A Perfect Fit

Paul Kool

iUniverse, Inc.
Bloomington

A Perfect Fit

iUniverse books may be ordered through booksellers or by contacting:

iUniverse
1663 Liberty Drive
Bloomington, IN 47403
www.iuniverse.com
1-800-Authors (1-800-288-4677)

ISBN: 978-1-4759-3629-2 (sc)
ISBN: 978-1-4759-3630-8 (e)

Printed in the United States of America

iUniverse rev. date: 07/13/2012

Chapter 1

Evie slinked her way along past the colorful displays of the shop windows on the freshly rain soaked Manhattan sidewalk in her handmade Italian pumps that although admittedly stylish, were taking on more water than the Titanic and producing a veritable symphony of slurp with each step.

Undaunted she pressed ahead looking trendy as always in a masterfully tapered wool three quarter fall coat, harvest colored pencil skirt, thin knit scarf draped *just so* to catch any breeze that happened by and a rain pelted semi-soggy cigarette hanging unapologetically from the corner of her mouth lending an ever so subtle hint of 'dockworker' to the ensemble.

She came to a halt in front of *Angelino's Fine Clothiers* display window; *Oh! – My! – God!'* she gasped and immediately began texting her friend Lena; "*At Angies... they still have the shoes Sue was talking about...TTL*"

This could be it she thought to herself; the perfect pair of shoes she had been searching for each Thursday on her lunch hour for the past two years; that unique combination of style, substance and comfort that every girl longs for in a shoe; and in a man for that matter.

Evie lit yet another cigarette and just stood there hopelessly lost in a shoe fantasy moment as she envisioned herself frolicking through breezy golden sun soaked meadows in slow motion in her new kicks never even once getting a heel stuck while all the little creatures of the forest as well as the bitchy girls from the secretarial pool gazed in wide wonder at her obviously superior style sense and high limit credit card.

"Yeeooouch!"

She had completely forgotten about the cigarette she was holding while she was away enjoying her fantasy vacation in *high heel heaven*; and apparently it elected to burn her finger for the flagrant oversight.

She casually cast the smoldering butt to the ground, discretely unleashed an array of expletives that would make a sailor blush and then skillfully slayed the rogue ciggy with a single fatal stab of her pencil heel.

As she basked in the delight of her victory while assessing the collateral damage to her manicure a somewhat familiar voice found her ear amidst the cacophony of sounds that enveloped her there on the crowded downtown sidewalk.

"Whoaow, that's gotta hurt!"

'Gee do ya think doofie?' she thought to herself as she gracefully turned smiling like a girl in a shampoo commercial flipping her hair as if in slow motion while discretely reaching into her bag for a ciggy to replace the one she publicly executed seconds earlier.

"Oh Tom, it's you, what a pleasant surprise; how are you?"

"Ummm...I don't know...ok I guess."

It wasn't a trick question so she wasn't quite sure why he had such difficulty answering it. Perhaps he mistakenly assumed that when one is asked how they are doing one is required to actually be honest when in reality a simple and instantaneous knee-jerk *'Fine'* or reasonable facsimile would suffice as in reality people rarely expect or even want the truth when they ask a casual acquaintance that particular question; could be a can of worms and a real time waster.

Eve hoped he would just 'be a dear' and go the hell away so she could get some more nicotine into her system before going inside the store to try on the shiny hand crafted objects of her affection and perhaps also take a quick peek at the cute designer bag that hung like a hypnotists pendulum from the arm of the mannequin in the window.

Immediately recognizing that Evie was having a considerable amount of difficulty lighting her replacement ciggy Tom reached over and cupped his big callous scarred hands around hers to block the wind as she stuck out her neck like a goose to align her ciggy with the flame burning inside their newly constructed hand-cave while the rain beat her semi-curly doo into limp submission.

The ciggy cooperated perhaps intimidated by the fate its predecessor suffered and lit up without a struggle.

"Thanks Tom! You're a lifesaver!"

"Those goddamn things are gonna kill ya!"

Eve thought to herself; 'how enlightening doctor doofus; oh my mistake; you're actually not a doctor at all are you!' Eve knew full well that Tom was against smoking so naturally it was the perfect time to indulge in an amusing little game of catty passive aggression.

Accordingly, she took a particularly long intense drag of the cigarette, held in the smoke, then pursed her glamorously glossed lips and ever so slowly exhaled into the damp cool air within inches of Tom's face; and then with her head tilted back and eyes closed she released a haughty 'Ahhhhhh' that bordered on the erotic.

Despite her formidable acting job Tom wasn't affected in the slightest. He knew exactly what she was doing and he liked it. He found her catty defiance, stubborn streak and whimsical flair for the dramatic highly amusing and more than a little alluring.

If only the feeling were mutual.

Evie didn't like him at all...perhaps 'detested' is a more apt descriptor. She only smiled when he suddenly materialized out of nowhere like a sidewalk ninja to save her from her impending nic-fit because she felt silly about the ciggy incident…all of which he witnessed; the daydream, the burn, the Yeeooouch and the merciless assassination.

Her friend Susan had introduced the pair weeks before at Tom's request after seeing Evie from across the room one evening at a local nightclub. Susan had known Tom since his arrival in New York City years earlier; his uncle and her father worked together so Susan felt somewhat compelled to play matchmaker and convince Evie to go out with him just once.

It was more than just a matter of doing a family friend a favor. Sue wholeheartedly believed that the two of them would make a cute couple and more than anything else she genuinely wanted to see her dear old friend Evie happy after the difficult times she had endured since childhood.

After months of pestering, Eve finally gave in and went on the date which she later reported to Susan as being a complete fiasco citing a lack of chemistry between the two as the culprit for the purportedly lost evening and politely asked Sue to stop nagging her further about him.

However, Eve's interpretation wasn't quite consistent with the facts as in reality Tom did everything a guy would be expected to do on a first date according to the proverbial dating handbook; he was courteous, punctual, presented flowers, opened doors for her and appeared to be genuinely interested in whatever she had to say.

But he was a blue collar worker and that apparently was somewhat of a point of contention for Eve despite the fact that most of the so called 'professional' guys that she had dated actually fared worse in the protocol department than Tom did.

Not that they were overtly rude or anything but to varying degrees, definitely somewhat inconsiderate and self-absorbed…and for the most part just plain dull. Conversely, not even Eve could say that Tom was devoid of a sense of humor as he had actually made her laugh more than a few times during their date…but this of course changed nothing.

"So listen, Sue's havin a party Friday night…pick you up at eight?" Tom said in a matter of fact tone sounding as if her acceptance was a foregone conclusion almost as if he would be doing her a favor by taking her along.

She didn't like the sound of the proposal any better than he did; he didn't mean it that way; it just came out wrong. He was actually a sincere humble guy that just got nervous and flubbed his proposal for some reason; something that rarely ever happened to him when asking a girl out.

But ultimately, in this particular instance it wouldn't have mattered if he recited a sonnet written specifically for the occasion by William Shakespeare himself as she had already decided their fate before the date ever took place.

Evie puffed her cigarette one final time before responding to his invitation in hopes of gaining a few extra seconds to invent a suitable excuse but unfortunately all she could come up with on short notice was a clumsily delivered;

"Oh I really wish I could go Tom but I have sooo much work to catch up on I'll probably be stuck in the office most of the evening; new clients; you know how it is."

He nodded nonchalantly in agreement but in fact didn't know *how it is* because he didn't have an office and he didn't have clients because he was a City Works Department worker … sewers to be more specific.

He spent his workday underground in dirty rat infested dimly lit service tunnels and subway stations fixing broken water mains and electrical cables and such; places that most people would never see or be remotely interested in visiting let alone working.

Despite his blue-collar status and contrary to the obvious stereotyping associated with individuals that do that kind of work he wasn't stupid by any means and picked up on Evie's shallow and poorly disguised snub immediately.

He did his best to remain cool and pretended that he was completely unaffected by her rebuff but his attempt at damage control was as badly delivered as Evie's snub. She could plainly see it on his face; the forced antithetical smile that totally conflicts with the rejection that always appears in the eyes and can't be hidden unless one is a sociopath or an award winning actor; neither of which applied to Tom.

He wasn't even a good liar; honest almost to a fault at times but by the same token he certainly wasn't what one would consider gullible or naïve either. Some call it *small town sensibility.*

Despite Evie's apparent lack of desire to pursue a relationship with Tom she did feel bad on some level for the poorly delivered snub...she wasn't without conscience. But what was she supposed to do? Just go with him anyway and lead him on? That wasn't her style.

And speaking of style, Evie had more than most.

Just about anything she wore looked good on her slim curvaceous five foot nine inch fine-boned frame. And her searing blue eyes and olive complexion produced a stunning and potent concoction of feminine pulchritude that could cast a powerful love-spell on any man... but she wasn't interested in just 'any man'...she was looking for Mr. Right...a perfect fit!

Evie of course was fully aware of her own beauty but always felt the need to act as if she was somehow oblivious to it and felt awkward when complimented by men or women; as if she was being labeled, summed up in an instant and immediately discounted as having nothing to offer beyond that.

When she was little her mother used to say *"Evie! God gave you a gift; use it!"* But somehow Evelyn was never even remotely flattered by that comment or the sentiment it conveyed.

Conversely she was never quite sure what exactly it was that her mother was implying when she said it; and ultimately she wasn't interested in knowing. The implicit negative and somewhat lascivious connotation was hard to ignore nonetheless and did little to improve her low sense of self-esteem.

As Evie and Tom stood there in the rain on the sidewalk, Tom, secretly feeling like a pariah at that point said *"Well, I guess I'll catch ya later then"*

'Oh goody, I can hardly wait' Evie thought to herself but instead smiled and said *"Thanks again Tom, it was so nice to see you"* graciously dismissing him.

He shot a smile back and walked away with an easily detectable fake spring in his step thrown in for good measure compliments of his wounded male ego in hopes of cleverly disguising the fact that he had just been emotionally obliterated.

Despite being snubbed, and acutely aware of the obvious but seemingly unfounded distain Evie harbored for him, Tom really liked her; unfortunately his friends didn't.

Two of them had met Evie the night of their date and although captivated by her beauty thought she was the worst kind of snob; one from a poor rural blue collar background that somehow made good in the big city and had conveniently forgotten where she came from and in the process…who she really was.

But Tom remained steadfast and would defend her, maintaining his belief that there was more to her than meets the eye; a sensitive caring person with a good heart underneath all the makeup, superficial corporate banter, contrived big city non-regional dialect, razor sharp sarcasm, expensive clothes and standoffish controlling behavior.

Essentially he saw her as a frightened little girl from the country dressed up in 'corporate Barbie attire' lost in the big city looking for something that she wouldn't recognize if it bit her on the B-Hinde and left a business card!

Of course he didn't base his beliefs on the one date; he had engaged in numerous and lengthy conversations about Evie with Susan so he knew quite a bit about her before the infamous date ever took place; including her preference for professional men, the status of which he hoped would change after their date but sadly didn't.

Tom certainly wasn't under the delusion that he was irresistible to women but he was well aware of the fact that most women did seem to find him quite attractive; and how could they not? Standing an even slim and muscular six feet tall with thick dark wavy hair and soft brown eyes he was quite striking in an unrefined way.

All in all he was a great catch for any woman; except apparently the one woman he was completely smitten with; Evie.

Sue and all her friends were totally mystified by the fact that she didn't at the very least find Tom irresistibly sexy and worthy of the occasional proverbial romp in the hay. Evie wouldn't even entertain the notion.

Tom was a hard working mid-western farm boy that came to New York City seven years prior; not to search for fortune and fame under the bright lights of the big city but to take the 'Subterranean Infrastructural Systems and Logistics Technician' (sewer/tunnel worker) job his uncle, a supervisor with the City Works Department, arranged for him.

He loved his job and felt that he was making a valid contribution to the welfare of the city; after all, people need water and electricity and functioning subway trains and it was his job to make sure those systems remained intact even if it meant being waist deep in poopy water on occasion. He took his duties just as seriously as any corporate executive took theirs.

But despite his love for his chosen trade there were times he would think about leaving the tunnels and trying to find an office job…maybe something in sales… but he detested the thought of having to participate in the superficiality of it all; the pretentious banter at the water cooler, the office politics, the backstabbing and having to be nice to people that he didn't care for all in the name of business and money. It was all just 'corporate bullshit' as far as he was concerned.

And the thought of sitting in a chair all day talking on the phone or typing on a computer was out of the question; woman's work! He liked the feeling of working with his hands and coming home tired and dirty at the end of the day to a man sized dinner….real American fare, not the miniscule ridiculously expensive portions of visually unidentifiable foods he'd never heard of served to the corporate crowd at the upscale Manhattan eateries.

After a good dinner he'd round out his day with a hot shower, a walk with his dog Eddy in the park near his little house in Queens; then watch a little television; preferably a good documentary or movie followed by the news and then indulge in a well-earned good night's rest.

A simple uncomplicated life for the most part; all he needed was a special lady to share it with; in reality he hadn't fared any better in the search for a life-mate than Evie had.

But that aside there was an even bigger stumbling block that deterred him from office work and that was the thought of having to put on a suit and tie every day. Certainly he looked great on those rare occasions he did have to put one on but it just wasn't his style.

It just never felt right; the ties choked him and he would constantly tug at his collar. The shoes felt odd and uncomfortable and the pants never felt like they fit properly; entirely too many layers of clothing...totally impractical the way he saw it. Being comfortable was far more important...more sensible.

The last time he wore a suit was at his mother's funeral. She had passed away after a lengthy and painful battle with cancer a year before he came to New York to take the sewer job his uncle arranged. He loved his mother dearly and her untimely passing took a considerable toll on him. He had hoped he would never have to wear a suit again.

Ultimately the only reason he occasionally mildly entertained the notion of an office job and compulsory induction into the *Armani brigade* was that 'suit and tie guys' seemed to be the only type of guys Evie would date with any regularity.

He often wondered if being one of them might help open the door if ever so slightly to Evie's seemingly impenetrable defenses…just long enough for her to see who he really was…not who she assumed he was.

Tom had also wondered why it was that none of those supposedly successful professional guys lasted more than a few months with Evie at least according to what Susan had told him previously. What was the problem? They made good money, had nice cars, dressed well but still didn't make the cut; none of it made any sense to him.

Finally after much deliberation Tom came to the realization that it all came down to a simple matter of Evie trying to land the right fish in the wrong pond; he wasn't prepared to try and become someone other than who he was for her or anyone. He believed that until she came to terms with who she was she'd remain in the wrong pond.

Growing up in a small rural farming community had definitely colored Evie's perception somewhat in terms of what she expected an acceptable suitor or potential mate to be; in particular anyone that doesn't drive a pickup truck and go to work in jeans, construction boots and a t-shirt and use the phrase 'Ya got that right!'

She had more than her fill of *pick-'em-up-truck* jerks growing up as she had dated plenty of them during high school and didn't want any part of that again. Their foul mouths, inability to control their hands and their arcane Neanderthal patriarchal ideals simply repulsed her. She thought they were nothing more than a bunch of misogynists and she didn't want any part of them.

What she wanted was a professional man; someone kind, considerate, educated and from a good family that could match, rival or exceed her formidable intellectual prowess and incontrovertible gift for creativity. In short, a man that knew what the word misogynist meant and how to spell it.

After Tom turned and walked away Evie made a b-line for the door of Angelino's and tried on the shoes. Unfortunately they didn't feel right so she just bought the bag instead and trotted off back to the office.

Chapter 2

"Excuse me Evie, Rena Lancaster is on line one and Mr. Ballantine wants to see you in his office when you get a moment...nice bag by the way...new?"

Eve looked up from her desk and said *"Just got it ....want this old one?"* as she continued to transfer the contents. By Eve's standards 'old' meant two or three months.

"You bet I do!"

"Done; here you go; enjoy!"

"Thank you so much Eve" Gail whispered as she clutched the bag and trotted off towards the door leaving Eve to her business call apparently thrilled to be inheriting yet another one of Eve's bags; her 'designer hand me downs' were the perks that made the job worthwhile for Gail.

Rena! Dahling! I was just thinking about you and was going to call you this afternoon to touch base...how are you?"

Despite Evie's ostensible enthusiasm she had no intention whatsoever of calling Rena and hated talking to her but she was cornered; Gail had already told her she was in and had transferred the call so Eve had no choice but to take it.

Rena only called when there was a problem or she wanted to make changes to the advertising campaign Evie put together for her; always more suggestions or concerns or something or other...never anything particularly constructive.

She could have referred Rena to her partner on the campaign, Mike Dubrow, but she didn't. She felt obligated as it was a huge account and brought in a ton of revenue for the firm. And she also wanted to ensure that things were handled accordingly, woman to woman, so she preferred to deal with Rena personally... keep her on a short leash.

This of course was no reflection on Mike. He was more than capable of handling Rena or any client without any assistance from anyone. Moreover, he was always respectful of Evie's considerable creative prowess and unlike some of the other young male execs in the company he never made the mistake of assuming that he knew more about the business or possessed more creative prowess than Evie did simply because she is a woman.

Apparently that type of arcane patriarchal thinking is as pervasive in the city as it is in small towns.... perhaps even more so...but for some reason Evie failed to recognize it or at the very least, acknowledge or accept it. But she was good at breaking down barriers in her professional life so this didn't present the slightest difficulty for her.

Mike was from a wealthy family in Boston; a graduate of the much revered Harvard Business School and was every bit as good-looking as Tom but in perhaps a more refined sense; finer facial features, straight sandy color hair neatly cut short and slightly spiked, steely blue eyes, slight svelte build all accentuated and enhanced by a veritable arsenal of tailored suits; Italian handmade shoes and a collection of ties that cost more than most men's entire wardrobes.

Dispensing with the obvious question; the answer is no; despite his love affair with fashion and his obvious preoccupation with his own appearance, he wasn't gay. Quite the contrary; he loved women ...every chance he got in fact, and went through them like the dozens of expensive suits and pairs of shoes he owned in his ever expanding collection.

'Maestro Mike' as his closest friends nicknamed him one drunken poker evening after relaying the details of his latest female conquest, considered his clothes to be a tool of sorts; a suit of armor or uniform he would wear not only in the boardroom but also in the nightclubs; essentially wherever attractive young ladies were to be found. But make no mistake; he wasn't a predator; he was a lady magnet.

But above all else he was a student of human nature and as such, knew perfectly well that women are at least initially attracted to well-dressed and impeccably groomed men...just enough to open the window of opportunity to close the deal with his wit and those bright blue eyes of his.

The Maestro also possessed considerable intellectual and perceptual abilities and this in and of itself provided him with a definitive performance advantage over his male peers at the firm. More precisely it served him well in determining the single most important factor in delivering a superior ad campaign; the fine art of bullshitting!

Mike and Tom couldn't have been more different. But they had one thing in common; they were both deeply '*in like*' with Evie and falling towards the '*in love*' side of the equation a little more each day.

Tom, who didn't have the gift of gab at least the way Mike did, wasn't making any progress at all with Evie. Mike on the other hand had been chipping away at her armor for quite some time slowly but steadily gaining her trust more each day...and of course he had a distinct advantage in terms of access as he saw her at work each day.

Despite the maestro's reputation as the office Casanova he was essentially a good hearted young man despite his overactive libido and worked very hard to produce the best results possible for his clients.

He also genuinely cared for Evie and had sensed that she felt the same for him but was experiencing a serious case of trepidation that could be solely attributed to his reputation. She knew of several women that he dated and didn't want to end up as the latest flavor of the month.

"Ok, Rena, lovely chatting as usual…don't hesitate to call if you have any questions at all"

Evie hung up the phone, shook her head and whispered 'Silly bitch!' But it was mission accomplished; she had managed to stave off yet another meeting to hear more of Rena's supposed thoughts on the campaign and what they could be doing better to boost sales.

Evie was of the unspoken belief that if Rena wanted a better campaign she should make a better product and put competent managers on it instead of poking her own inept nose into the works endlessly.

She considered Rena to be a pushy self-absorbed egomaniacal over-privileged twit with more money than imagination or creative ability who was fortunate enough to have inherited a business from her father that she essentially knew nothing about, nor really cared about beyond her feeble esoteric attempts to convey the perception that she was in control of the company's destiny….more a matter of self-importance and style versus substance…a 'poser' for lack of a better word.

According to Evie the only thing Rena ever did right was to hire her and her firm to handle the account. Having Evie and her boundless wit and imagination at the helm of the campaign had been a wise choice and was clearly reflected every fiscal quarter when Rena's financials were released to salivating stockholders.

It all came easily for Evie. From the time she was a child she was enthralled with advertising; she of course didn't understand what it was at the time but she loved to watch the commercials on TV and walk around the house singing the various jingles from all the commercials; and she could sing or recite any one of them on demand at any time. This ability always provided a source of amusement for Eve and her girlfriends.

She would also clip out advertisements from magazines and newspapers and create collages on her bedroom walls with them. It was a preoccupation that concerned her mother; she thought it was unhealthy and just plain odd but didn't realize that it provided Evie with a safe haven and escape from the constant bickering of her parents and the sounds of various objects being hurled in anger on a regular basis throughout the house.

Unfortunately neither of Evie's parents had the wherewithal to realize what their fighting was doing to her or to see beyond their own selfish interests and agendas. But it was what it was….beyond Evie's control. She didn't like that feeling.

When Evie was twelve her father, a long-haul truck driver, finally left after years of turmoil in the house and she had seen him only a handful of times since then as he had remarried and had three children with his new wife whom he eventually also divorced years later. Perhaps he was fishing in the wrong pond as well.

He was essentially a good man and had called Evie several times over the years particularly on her birthday and Christmas and so forth but Evie would never agree to see him and still wouldn't. She still blamed him.

Nonetheless, after he left, her mom started drinking even more than she already was and started dating local guys that saw her as nothing more than a goodtime barfly. She just couldn't see past that; it was her present and her future all rolled up into one ball of confusion and emotional desolation…a life without living…a pointless existence.

Sometimes she'd sneak a few dollars out of one of her date's pockets after he had passed out drunk and use it to buy food for her and Evie. Her father sent money regularly but the problem was that it quickly disappeared at the local bars and the liquor store without his knowledge. That money was intended to provide food and clothing mainly for Evie.

Evie's mother's drinking continued even after Evie went away to college on a scholarship. She always dreaded having her mother visit as she would always show up with her latest flavor of the week boyfriend or some idiot she picked up in a bar the night before still half-drunk stinking of booze and cigarettes and wearing fashions and hairstyles that were clearly inappropriate for a woman of her age.

It was as if she was stuck in a time warp and hadn't noticed that the world had changed, years had passed and that she had aged. The alcohol kept her in a subconsciously self imposed emotional and physical exile from her own life; or rather the life she could have been living if she'd put forth the slightest bit of effort to extricate herself from the misery and dependency that controlled and continued to debilitate her.

Some of the other students from apparently 'good homes' would laugh at Evie behind her back and talk about her incessantly even when she was present. Their cruel and catty comments wounded Evie time and time again but those kids didn't realize just how determined and resourceful she could be when provoked.

And in turn Eve couldn't understand why kids from such supposedly good homes could turn out to be such shitty people; back then the definition of 'good home' was represented by one number; total assets…the higher the better apparently. No one ever apparently questioned the correlation.

But she endured and thrived in the face of adversity. She learned to be strong and independent at an early age and had become nothing short of an unstoppable force in college consistently earning top marks and academically annihilating her adversaries with the greatest of ease.

Unfortunately it seemed that no matter how many steps forward she took, a single visit to the dorm by her mother would set her back two steps.

On one particular visit over the Christmas holidays her mom Lucy showed up at the college and was so drunk that she fell down the stairs and earned herself a trip to the hospital; and the nickname 'Lucy goosey the lush' which the mean girls would chant anytime they saw Eve.

Eve's friends, particularly Susan always tried to stand up for her but she insisted that she would take care of the matter herself in her own time after graduation as she didn't want any blemishes on her school record which of course might hinder her ability to get a job.

A month after graduation she approached the mean girls and offered to take them to lunch to clear the air between them before she left for New York to start her new life.

They all accepted, had a lovely meal and drinks and then a lovely episode of diarrhea afterwards courtesy of the laxative that Eve had the waiter, a friend of hers, slip into their food. Eve got on a bus to New York an hour later and never looked back!

But as usual the cause of all the problems wasn't the mean girls; or even her mother; Eve always attributed it all to her father for not being there for her mother.

She was as concerned about her mother as she was ashamed of what she had become. It was one of those situations where love and hate have to coexist in the same relationship and one consistently offsets the other to varying degrees yet there is little one can do to improve the apparent discrepancy without risking losing the relationship altogether or avoid getting lost in the emotional abyss that exists between love and hate. This is the worst kind of relationship.

But despite it all she did love her mom deeply and on some level understood the pain she went through after her father left but at the same time blamed her for not taking control of her own destiny; but blamed her less than her dad; so needless to say it was a mess.

Eve often wondered why her mother was so incapable of taking charge of her own life; as after all, Evie was experiencing precisely the same sense of loss and betrayal herself over her father's departure from their lives.

Instead of drinking and running around with strange men young ambitious Evelyn pulled herself together, left that small town and made a name for herself in New York at one of the most prestigious advertising firms in the city.

"Oh crap! I wonder what Ballantine wants; I hope it has nothing to do with Rena's account; I'm not making any changes...that silly bitch always tries to go over my head when I say no to her stupid ideas" she said to Gail as she closed the door to her office and clicked along the marble floored hallway to Mr. Ballantine's office.

It was a false alarm; nothing to do with Rena. Apparently Ballantine just wanted to touch base on a couple of other accounts and sit in on one of the brainstorming meetings they were to have later that day.

Evie left the office at five sharp for a dinner date with her girlfriends at a trendy eatery in the Village.

Chapter 3

Susan pushed her way through the crowded restaurant to the table Evie and Lena were already seated at.

"Sorry I'm late; took me twenty minutes to get a cab; did you already order?"

"No" Evie replied *"we're still having drinks"*

"I'm famished...do you guys mind if we order soon?" Susan asked.

Evie and Lena nodded in agreement and signaled the waiter.

"Wow...I love your scarf Sue; where did you get that?" Evie said reaching over the table to feel the soft material with her impeccably manicured fingers, the tiny burn mark now almost gone, as the waiter arrived to take their dinner orders.

Evie obviously had a formidable fashion sense but she openly acknowledged that Susan's was even keener and that being the case didn't mind shamelessly 'borrowing' ideas for ensembles from her; and Susan, a stunningly beautiful plus size gal and Eve's oldest and dearest friend was always flattered when asked by Evie for fashion advice and opinions.

The girls ordered.

"Wow, he's a cutie Evie" Lena said while watching the waiter as he walked away.

"How would you know, you haven't looked at his face yet."

"Very funny..."

Then Lena said *"Eve, why don't you give the poor guy your number; he's been watching you since the minute we walked through the door."*

"How about I don't! Hello! Just in case you guys haven't noticed yet; He's a waiter! And that adds up to no future, no money, and most certainly no honey!"

Susan cut in; *"Is that domestic or imported honey?"*

They all laughed as Susan continued;

"Ok, so waiter guy doesn't make the cut; we get it! Now let's move onto a more interesting topic; the topic of super cutie Mikey...so?"

Lena and Susan both leaned in and were staring at Evie in anticipation of good news and all the romantic details they could handle to satisfy their hunger.

"Careful girls, you're drooling" Evie chuckled.

"So tell Evie...has he asked you out yet or is he still beating around the bush and stalking you like some big sexy beast in the jungle waiting to pounce"

"Sounds yummy" Susan said as they all giggled along.

"Sorry girls...nothing to report yet. Every time I look at him his eyes are screaming 'I wanna take you home and make love to you' but his mouth isn't saying anything... at least not the things I want to hear like 'Evie, come away with me, let's leave this place forever and fly off to a desert island where we can live on nothing but our love for all of eternity"

"Hey that was really good Evie...you really do have a way with words girl"

"That's why they pay me the mediocre buck's kid"

"But really Evie, if he's going to be such a chicken shit then why don't you help him a little by asking him if he'll come to my party with you tomorrow night?"

Evie looked horrified and said *"You're joking right?"*

Susan laughed *"No I'm not joking...and why not? This is 2012 you know...we're not in the dark ages anymore! Women ask guys out all the time"*

"Well I don't! And furthermore I expect that if a guy likes me he'll have to just get over his shyness and tell me what's on his mind...IF anything at all!" Evie proclaimed sitting there in defiance rummaging through her purse looking for the pack of cigarettes that was right under her nose on the table.

Lena suddenly jumped up *"Shit! I gotta pee...when I come back who wants to go to the room?"*

"I'll come with you...anyone seen my cigarettes?" (Evie)

*"Look down!" (*Susan)

"Wow, really?" Evie said while shaking her head in disbelief and getting up to join Lena slightly embarrassed at her apparent state of preoccupation.

After a brief trip to the ladies room the girls arrived at *The Room* as everyone called it; the designated smoking area at the back of the restaurant. It was an imposing little space decorated in 'Early American Prison' with a huge bucket size ashtray and one window facing the inside of the restaurant and another with bars on it that afforded a positively disturbing panoramic view of the alley and all the lascivious activity that often went on out there.

But no one that frequented *the room* ever cared; firstly, they were New Yorkers and had seen it all before and secondly; they were just grateful they had a place they could light-up and satisfy their voracious ciggy addictions before and after their meals, even if it was reminiscent of a suite at Rikers Island.

The girls puffed away and chatted for a few minutes and another girl came in; a beautiful petite blonde with a voluptuous figure and striking green eyes.

"Hey gals" she said gravel voiced but cheerily as she walked in to join the girls with a pack of smokes in hand

ready to indulge in a little chemical warfare; a battle she was clearly losing judging from the raspy sound coming from her throat when she spoke. Yes indeed, she had the face of an angel and the voice of a truck driver.

"Phew! Doesn't the fuckin' fan work in here?"

Apparently she also had the mouth of a truck driver!

She waved her hand in the air as if to make a little smoke-free cave in the corner of the room that she could step into and then pollute with her own fresh unique blend of toxic airborne chemicals.

The thick cigarette smoke swirling around the tiny room permeated their hair and clothing creating a unique olfactory concoction that when combined with their various brands of perfumes produced a 'bouquet de stench' more befitting a brothel or bar by the docks than an upscale eatery in Manhattan. Simply put; they looked like candy and smelled like crap!

Lena and Evie just smiled in response to Samantha's comment but offered no commentary of their own. They were already lit up and in a state of nicotine and formaldehyde induced bliss as they puffed and stared aimlessly into space while trying to fill up their respective smoke caves.

"Oh- my- God!" Lena whispered excitedly while peering through the window into the restaurant;

"There's that guy Tom, the one that Susan introduced you to (she latched onto Evie's arm)*...ooh shit...he's*

29

looking this way....and he's got a rose in his hand...how sweet...it's probably for you"

"Shit!" Evie snapped with an utter look of terror on her face worthy of an award from the horror movie maker's guild. But she quickly regained her composure and said *"Don't worry...he doesn't smoke...he hates it! He won't come in here!"*

"You know, (Lena said with head tilted to one side as she watched Tom standing at the bar) *he's super cute... nice bod Mr. Sewer guy. Meeeow! What's wrong with you girl? You guys would look totally adorable together!"*

Evie raised her eyebrows;

"Come on, just look at him Lena; it speaks for itself; he's wearing jeans and a t-shirt with a sport jacket for Christ sake! And it gets even worse; look down... see that?...those are construction boots...I can't date someone that dresses like that."

Lena proclaimed *"First of all, I think the construction boots look adorable...kind of rugged and manly but you're totally missing the point; it doesn't matter what he looks like in clothes; it matters what he looks like without them; and I bet he looks just fine!"*

Evie laughed, slightly embarrassed by her bold comment and in particular the meowing and ooo-ing and ahh-ing that accompanied it;

"You're a dirty girl, do ya know that? But if you promise to behave I'll tell you about seeing him at lunch"

Lena's eyes opened wide at the prospect and listened intently as Evie continued;

"Well not 'seeing' seeing him...you know what I mean; remember when I texted you from Angelino's at lunch? Just before I went in to buy this? (Pointing at the bag hanging from her shoulder) *...I was looking at the bag through the window...well, the shoes Susan mentioned at first and then I noticed the bag but anyway that's when Doofie popped up out of nowhere and asked me if I wanted to go to Sue's party with him tomorrow night; can you imagine?....the boy just doesn't get it; I'm not interested! And after that horrible and boring first date we had you'd think he would have got the point but I guess they aren't too bright back wherever the hell he comes from; Anyway, so I just made up an excuse to get out of it and said I had a lot of work to catch up on* (she started talking even faster) *Oh crappers...he's coming this way, oh no, I hope to God he doesn't ask me out again...maybe he followed us here...ewww, that would be creepy...what if he's a stalker or something? But I don't want him to embarrass himself again...or me for that matter...especially here...they know me!"*

Lena tightening her grip on Evie's arm as if waiting for the moment of impact during a meteor storm.

"Shit shit shit...how do I look?" Evie said while primping her hair.

You look fine and what do you care anyway?" Lena said.

Evie didn't answer.

Just then Tom opened the door to the smoking room.

Evie and Lena pretended to be surprised to see him as he said "*Hey girls...wow...I didn't expect to see you guys here* (waiving one hand in the air to fan the clouds of smoke away and holding the rose in the other) ...*Man, how can you stand it in here?*"

"*Make a cave*" Lena blurted.

"*A what?*"

"*Oh never mind!*" Evie said as she extended her right arm to accept the rose with a big fake shiny grin as if about to receive an Academy Award before walking off the stage in the wrong direction like a spatially challenged chimp.

Unfortunately Tom walked right past her.

"*I see you guys have met my friend Samantha*" he said as he leaned in towards her, presented her with the single red rose and gave her a gentle kiss on the cheek.

Evie looked every bit as ridiculous as she felt; not only because of her obviously mistaken assumption regarding the rose but even more so because she had just been slagging Tom right in front of his date!

There was little Eve could do to make amends or look like less of an imbecile so she just stood there and said nothing as if she might suddenly invoke her super powers of evaporation and dematerialize into the smoke filled air; she had to settle for super-embarrassment.

Tom, obviously unaware of what had been said in the smoking room prior to his arrival bid Lena and Evie farewell and headed back into the restaurant leaving Samantha with the girls, rose in hand, to finish her cigarette before joining him inside for dinner.

"Oh my God I'm so sorry Samantha. I didn't know you were with Tom...I don't know what to say; I feel just horrible!"

Samantha just smiled like an angel and then unleashed a sarcastic gravel voiced verbal fireball that had the velocity and intent of an assassin's bullet;

"Oh don't be sorry sweetie and don't worry, I won't say anything to him about this...I don't talk about people behind their backs like some people...and honey, by the way, you have no idea what you're missing when those big construction boots of his come off!"

Samantha strode past Evie slightly nudging her with her shoulder on her way out with her nose in the air.

Evie just stood there unable to speak for a full two or three minutes obviously trying to figure out how she could downplay the incident.

Finally she blurted out; *"Oh my God! What a whore! Ewww...and he had the unmitigated gall to ask me out when he dates girls like that? Yuk...so dirty!! Let's collect Sue and get out of here!"*

Evie and Lena went back to the table to find Susan voraciously devouring a huge plate of wings and a salad the size of a Buick on the side. She looked up between bites and said *"I thought you guys had left or something. Sorry, I just couldn't wait any longer!"*

Evie and Lena still in a state of shock just sat there while Susan came up for air once again;

"Oh this is sooo good. I've been famished all afternoon... this diet is killing me...the hell with it... (reaching for yet another dinner roll and more salad) *...truth be told I'd rather be a little chubby and a lot happy than skinny and miserable...not that you two toothpicks are miserable or anything."*

Lena responded jokingly;

"Nope, no reason to be miserable here at all; I'm going to be thirty next month and live alone with two cats"

The girls all laughed of course but the moment was disturbingly prophetic.

Evie had lost her appetite but signaled the waiter for another drink. All the while Samantha kept looking over at Eve deliberately laughing and throwing her hair back to ensure that she knew what a great time she was having with Tom.

And just for good measure she would pull him close every couple of minutes to whisper something in his ear and then flip her hair and start laughing incessantly again and then give him a series of little love pecks on the lips and cheek.

It absolutely infuriated Evie!

Why? She had no idea. But she needed to even the score! It was time for action Evie style!

She got up, went to the bar and ordered a huge ice cold pitcher of draught beer; then casually walked over to Tom's table smiling like a Cheshire cat at a mouse convention and proceeded to dump the entire contents of the pitcher over Samantha's head from behind.

Samantha's pretty dress, which she no doubt bought especially for the occasion, was ruined and her long flowing mane was a mass of beer soaked tangles. She smelled like a brewery…which was a definite step up from the combination of cigarette smoke and perfume.

Evie then proceeded to put on a performance worthy of an Academy Award;

"Oh my gosh! I am so so sorry, please forgive me… something caught my heel and I tripped…here…let me help you (halfheartedly dabbing Samantha's hopelessly beer soaked shoulder) … *I feel so terrible about this"*

And then for the final encore, which she ensured everyone in the room could hear she blurted out in horror; "O*h no! Your hair extensions are all wet…let me take them out for you"* as she reached for Samantha's golden mane.

Samantha jumped up to run to the bathroom in tears while chuckles abounded from nearby tables from the male patrons which were just as quickly suppressed by the 'evil eye' they all received from their female companions for their apparent lack of sensitivity. In all likelihood none of those men had sex that night.

And then… the final *coup de gras!*

As Samantha strode past Evie on her way to the washroom Evie smiled and whispered *"That's how I roll Bitch!"* in Samantha's ear with all the intensity of a rattle snake striking and injecting its venom.

Tom didn't say a word. He was perfectly aware that Evie did this on purpose. He pretended to be mad and even put up his hand as if to say *"Stop! Don't even bother talking to me right now!"* when Evie tried to explain as part of her performance.

But secretly although Tom felt bad for his date he was unbelievably happy about the incident. Why? Because Evie reacted! It was a like sign from God; she was jealous! If she didn't care about him she never would have pulled that stunt.

Evie returned to her table cheery as ever. Apparently her remorse and sullen mood had vanished the very second Samantha left the room after the public beer baptism.

Eve smiled and proclaimed *"You know something girls, I've suddenly gotten my appetite back…"* while signaling for the waiter *"what say we eat, have a few more drinks and go dancing afterwards?"*

"Uh…hold on one little second missy! Umm, what was that?" Susan demanded.

"What?" Evie said angelically.

"That...over there....the beer...that whole thing" Susan continued, obviously confused as she didn't know about the exchange of pleasantries in the smoking room earlier or the sudden Jekyll and Hyde routine Evie just performed for the crowd.

As Tom and Samantha were leaving he made a point of looking back across the room at Evie. Susan felt embarrassed and just shrugged her shoulders so Tom wouldn't think she had anything to do with it.

Then he looked directly at Eve and shook his head as if to appear disappointed and angry just for posterity. Evie smiled. He winked.

Susan was getting very impatient at that point;

"Ok...what the fuck was that...again with the games... and what did I just see go on between you and Tom... that was a moment you two just had there...he winked at you"

"He probably just had something in his eye...there was no 'moment' as you put it, I assure you...Tom and I... please...how many drinks have you had my dear?... you're cut off!" she said laughing.

"Oh my God...Evie ...I saw it...it was a moment alright; you saw it too right Lena?" Susan asked looking for consensus and validation.

"What? Sorry..." Lena said conveniently acting confused. She was cleverly employing the 'duh' method of sensitive topic avoidance used often by men; she

grew up with three brothers and as such was more than familiar with their anti-emotionality tactics.

The truth was she saw 'the moment' as well but didn't want to get between Susan and Evie or have to choose sides in their friendly but highly charged debate.

Susan, visibly frustrated by that point just said '*oh never mind!*" and left the subject.

Evie could see her friend getting frustrated and possibly feeling left out and possibly a little put off by the way Eve just treated her friend Tom so Eve obliged and proceeded to explain the entire situation to her in detail.

A plate of spaghetti and three drinks later Susan was up to speed and giddy as a school girl because she could see what Tom saw regardless of Evie's refusal to entertain the notion; Evie had a secret *thing* for terrible Tom the sewer guy whether Eve realized it or not.

Chapter 4

It was a big day for Evie. And it was a big day for Mike as well. There was an important client with a potential multimillion dollar account flying in from Los Angeles to meet them both for dinner to hear what they had come up with in terms of an advertising strategy.

To say the least there was an enormous amount of money and prestige at stake...they had one shot at the proverbial 'brass ring' or the account would be lost to another firm within twenty four hours.

Evie and Mike had been preparing for the long awaited meet for weeks and they were more than ready. They had put together an ad campaign that encompassed radio, TV and print media for the client who owned a highly successful sportswear and casual clothing line with distributorship throughout America and Canada looking to expand into the European markets.

The client's company *"Fastrack Wear"* was a definite up and comer. It was geared towards young to middle aged well paid executives who were in essence on the 'fast track' and interested in both style and quality and didn't mind paying a little extra for it; essentially people like Mike and Evie themselves.

The fact that they fit the target demographic to a tee provided the young marketing whizzes a definitive edge in putting together the campaign.

Mr. Luzon, the CEO, owner and founder felt that the advertising firm he had been using in Los Angeles over the past several years had lost sight of the objective, was out of fresh ideas and simply wasn't doing enough to get him the market share he demanded as expediently as he would have liked.

Not that the company wasn't doing well…it was doing very well indeed. But doing 'well' in the corporate arena is like settling for second best; like Evie's boss and co-owner of the ad firm Mr. Ballantine would often say;

"You're number one or you're number nothing!"

That never made any sense to Evie or Mike but it always sounded so philosophically profound whenever Ballantine would deliver it before battle to the troops in his brash inimitable style in the boardroom.

Luzon envisioned his company and its clothing line becoming a 'must have' staple in corporate circles worldwide within a two year timeframe and was counting on Evelyn and Mike to present fresh ideas that would facilitate the move to the coveted number one slot and leaving behind their apparent 'number nothing' slot…that's number two in real numbers.

Mike who was usually cool and collected was pacing back and forth like he often did before an important meeting with a new client. He never tried to hide it as he was of the opinion that a slight case of the nerves was a good thing; sharpens the senses and increases the drive to succeed he would always say.

"Eve lets go over this one more time…we've still got two hours before we meet Luzon at Camarillo's."

"Oh Mike stop! We've been over this campaign a million times; we created it remember?" she said laughingly as she leaned back in her chair crossing her long shapely legs coquettishly as her black pencil skirt slipped a little further up past her knees than she would normally allow it to.

But it was for a worthy cause; to get Mikes mind off the account for a few minutes so he could relax. And it worked nicely as he seemed to be having considerable difficulty keeping his eyes from wandering to her legs every few seconds; she knew it and decided to have a little fun with him;

"Mike! You were just looking at my legs weren't you!"

"Don't be silly, of course not!"

"Oh yes you were! Oh my, do I have a run in my nylons or something?" she said stretching out her right leg, pointing her toe, raising the hem of her skirt a few more inches and running her hand up and down the length of

her leg pretending to try and feel for a run in her ultra-sheer hose.

This of course was driving Mike insane with desire as he became flushed and nervous completely forgetting about Luzon and the business at hand. Mission accomplished.

"You're looking a little flushed Mikey...are you ok?"

For a guy that was purported to be, and in fact was the undisputed office Casanova Evie had little difficulty turning him into a blubbering mass of jelly within the space of about two minutes. She thought it was funny and was also flattered by his obvious desire for her.

"I'm just going to run to the washroom and splash some water on my face; it's a little hot in here"

"Feels fine to me" Evie said crossing her legs in the opposite direction this time. He left the room immediately. She chuckled to herself *"Men!"*

Mike left red faced but returned apparently composed. *"Ok let's go over this thing one more time...and stop the thing with the legs young lady...it's really distracting me..."*

"That's the point" Evie said laughing.

Then Mike caught on; *"Ok, I get it...smart girl...Mikey boy is too wound up and needs a distraction courtesy of the lovely miss Evie so he doesn't over-think the presentation and blow it....well done!"*

"Something like that yeah...but listen there's nothing more we can do with the campaign; it's good; in fact it's some of the best work we've done to date and you know it; we are as ready as we're going to be ...there isn't a question that Luzon could ask us that we can't answer so for God sake please relax"

"You're right! If this campaign doesn't do it for Luzon then nothing will. And yeah, I agree, it is some of our best work; I hope the son of a bitch appreciates it so we can just sign off on this deal and rollout the campaign... nice stems by the way"

"Ok tiger, save the charm for the client's wife!" Evie said chuckling.

In reality she was quite aroused by the little game of 'leg show' she had just played with Mike. She did her best to maintain a cool exterior but was quivering like a smitten schoolgirl on the inside and wanted him just as much as he wanted her but naturally kept it to herself.

Mike and Evie arrived at the restaurant a little early and ordered drink's at the bar because their table wasn't available yet. *"I'm going outside for a smoke Mike: wanna come?"*

"Actually, no, not right now; I'll stay here incase our boy arrives early; have one for me though! And whatever you do don't let him see you smoking; it won't look good...and take a mint or something afterwards so he doesn't smell it on your breath!"

"Do you know a guy named Tom by any chance?"

"Who?"

"Never mind!" Evie quipped as she trotted off on yet another pair of hellishly uncomfortable fabulous looking designer heels selected just for the occasion from the 'currently fashionable' shoe area of her closet which was like a miniature gated community for over privileged and unrealistically priced footwear.

They weren't the perfect pair of shoes she had been searching for but they were perhaps a close second; that's 'number nothing' in the context of both fashion and romance.

The important thing was that Evie got in the last word regarding the mint comment. It was important to her. She detested the thought of being told what to do by a man, even if she did have romantic notions about him.

Control was important to her but ironically it was precisely that control that had kept her from finding true love in the past; the inability to get out of her own way and listen to her heart instead of her stringent acceptable criteria list.

Mike downed a double Manhattan on the rocks and ordered another. As he waited for it a hand grasped his shoulder from behind;

"Hello Michael...business or pleasure?"

It was Sebastian. No one else called Mike by his given name except his mom.

He and Mike were bred of the same ilk; old money! Like Mike, he was from a wealthy family in Boston; born at the same hospital, lived in the same neighborhood and the two had been practically inseparable growing up and right through their university years at Harvard.

"*Doing a deal; client arriving soon; here with Evelyn*" Mike replied.

Sebastian contorted his face with disapproval; "*Disappointing....drinks later?*"

"*Perhaps*" Mike replied.

"*Call me!*" Sebastian said just before floating off into the abyss of patrons crowded shoulder to shoulder in the bar area of the restaurant.

Mike's Manhattan on the rocks appeared in front of him on the bar; he downed it and proceeded to go over the game plan in his head once more; his nerves had now disappeared; he was in the 'zone' and ready to do battle. Evie's earlier game of leggy distraction was exactly what he needed to help refocus.

A few moments later Evie appeared at the front door of the eatery with Mr. Luzon and his wife Ilea. Although Luzon was a man in his early fifties his wife was a mere child of twenty four in comparison; a Swedish sportswear model that was easily a half foot taller in heels than her husband.

Evie led the Luzon's over to Mike at the bar and made the formal introductions. Ilea looked at Mike like he

45

was a piece of candy that she wanted to take home and swallow whole.

The normal two second business handshake interval was extended at her insistence to at least fifteen seconds which made Mike more than a little uncomfortable; not because a pretty lady was holding his hand of course but because of whom that pretty lady happened to be and what was at stake that evening.

Evie recognized Ilea's interest in Mike immediately but was nothing if slightly amused by it and made a mental note to rib him about it later. But she wondered why Mr. Luzon failed to take note; that is until he jumped on the bandwagon himself and started telling Evie how beautiful he thought she was and that she really should meet him for a drink the next day at his hotel suite so he could get to know her a little better.

But ultimately it was the careful placement of his hand upon Evie's knee under the table intermittently accompanied by gentle squeezes and attempts to slowly slide his hand up her thigh that made his intentions abundantly clear.

By then it was obvious to young Evie and Mike that the Luzon's had an open marriage and were in all likelihood swingers...or wife swappers or whatever the acceptable term is for it.

Evie thought such arrangements were disgusting but wisely chose to keep her opinions in this regard to herself and steadfastly continued to stave off Luzon's ostentatious and unwelcome advances like a trooper.

It was almost like a comedy skit; you see one hand going under the table and another reaching down to push it away; then another and another; chairs being repositioned; changing of seats, walking around the table, all in Eve and Mike's valiant efforts to elude the clutches of their ardent amorous pursuers.

By the halfway point of the meeting Luzon and wife had given up on their attempts to woo the young ad exec's and they could all finally get down to the business at hand without further distraction.

By the end of the evening and multiple cocktails it was apparent that Luzon was impressed by the duo's ideas and informal presentation. For all intents and purposes they had a deal.

Just before Luzon left and they were all shaking hands he leaned forward towards Evie and Mike and said in a quiet enquiring voice while pointing his finger back and forth at the two; *"Are you two together?"*

"Together?" Mike said, obviously caught off guard.

"Yeah, you know ...together" as Luzon crossed two fingers to illustrate.

"Oh, you mean ...toooo-geth-rrrrr!! (Pause)... *no sir!"* Mike replied obviously embarrassed.

"Yezzzz...thhhhat's whhhhhat I mmmmmmeannnnt" Luzon shot back as if talking to someone with a debilitating head injury that prevents them from comprehending the meaning of words but recognize the sentiment conveyed by the tone and sound of the

word much like a dog would. They all began to laugh at the refreshing little interjection of levity.

Evie and Mike sat back down at the table after seeing the Luzon's off and opened another bottle of champagne to celebrate.

"Together....us?" (Mike)

"Yeah...imagine that huh?" (Evie)

"Yeah....imagine" (Mike)

"Silly!" (Evie)

"Absolutely ridiculous!" (Mike)

"You can kiss me now!" (Evie)

"Ok" (Mike)

And they did, for several minutes in fact.

When they took a breather Evie laughed and said while Mike poured her a glass of champagne; *"I think Ilea really likes you...I thought she was going to rip off her clothes and jump onto your lap at any moment...and since she was dressed like a low rate streetwalker I wouldn't have been a bit surprised!"*

"Ouch! Nasty!" Mike laughed and then continued *"but you're right; she kept playing footsie with me under the table and kept touching my leg; talk about awkward."*

"Oh come off it Mikey you loved every minute of it! My stars, it's not every day a 6 foot tall blonde Swedish

swim suit model, albeit one that dresses like a whore, comes onto you."

He leaned back in his chair and put on a deliberately arrogant facial expression with eyebrows raised and laughingly said *"Well as a matter of fact it happens at least twice a week...don't kid yourself!"*

"Keep dreaming mister!" she chuckled playfully as he joined her with his own infectious laugh.

But after a moment his tone became more sincere and somewhat serious as he looked into her eyes and said;

"Eve, I must say you were absolutely brilliant this evening; and that idea about the expansion to the London and Paris market by teaming up to show the line with big name designers at international runway shows on-line for corporate web-casts was a stroke of genius!"

She smiled like a Cheshire cat and said *"yeah, that was pretty good wasn't it; I just pulled that one out of my hat to get his attention back on topic...and his hand off my thigh"*

"Can you blame him? I mean that's a pretty wonderful looking leg you've got there...both of them in fact."

"Why Mr. Dubrow, you naughty boy, I had no idea you've been ogling my legs again...I'll have to be more careful from now on" Eve said in an obviously contrived but surprisingly convincing southern belle accent.

He moved to the chair next to her, took her hand and said *"Seriously, you are a wonderful girl Eve... from your beautiful legs to your baby blues, to your razor sharp wit...every inch of you is nothing short of stupendous!"*

They sat silently for a moment gazing into each other's eyes as if it was a case of love at first site. He took her hand squeezing it ever so slightly while the champagne gently swirled through both their heads as the people and the noise in the room around them magically faded away as if they were the only two people left on the planet.

They kissed again.

It wasn't a long kiss but it was soft and sensual; the kind of kiss that a girl longs for; the kind that makes her feel like hers are the only lips her man would ever want to taste every hour, every day, for the rest of his life.

They sat in silence for yet another moment just basking in the glow of the rapture that had enveloped them. It was by all accounts a beautiful rare moment that most people never have the good fortune to experience.

"So hey beautiful, how bout finishing this perfect evening with a nightcap out on my terrace overlooking the city skyline"

Evie, despite wanting to just jump in a cab with him that very second and rush to his apartment and surrender to him completely, managed to regain her composure somehow and keep her wits about her.

She reminded herself that he had a reputation as a Casanova for good reason; He was as smooth as the silk stockings she wore that night and as such didn't want to end up as nothing more than his latest conquest; she needed to figure out what it was he wanted before they went any further so she wouldn't end up being emotionally shredded. She wanted more and she deserved more.

She rolled her eyes, affectionately fiddled with his tie and said;

"Believe me Mikey I'd really like to have that nightcap but I know what's going to happen if I come home with you right now and I'm just not ready to jump into anything that quickly...I don't want us to do something we'll both regret in the morning"

She expected him to either become annoyed or pull out the heavy artillery and come at her with a full arsenal of brilliantly crafted lines designed to close the deal but he didn't.

He surprised her by concurring;

"Point taken Evie! I fully understand; I don't want to pressure you. So I tell ya what; why don't you come to my place on Friday night. I'll cook us a nice spaghetti dinner and we'll just talk, watch a little TV and just hang out; no hanky panky expected or required; just two people enjoying each other's company. ...so whaddaya say?"

"Well, I suppose a girl can't say no to an invitation like that so you've got yourself a date Mr. Dubrow...but no hanky panky... agreed?"

"Scouts honor!"

"You were never a scout"

"I know!"

After paying the bill they left in separate cabs after a long sensual embrace and kiss on the sidewalk outside the restaurant.

Sitting there alone in the cab on the way back to her apartment she couldn't help but question her decision. She almost felt guilty about denying Mike...and herself. Perhaps she should have just seized the moment and been impulsive for once in her life and gone home with him she mused.

She even considered having the driver take her to his building and just let fate take its course but she suddenly realized that she didn't know where he lived. Of course she could have called Mike on his cell phone to get the address but by then the sense of magic and impetuosity would have been lost.

As the cab wound its way through the city streets and the cool night air rushed in through her partially open window she experienced a moment of clarity and affirmation with regard to her decision.

She thought to herself *"No!...if he wants me he'll have to make the effort and be respectful of my feelings and thoughts where this relationship is concerned; I don't want to set any bad precedents...no mistakes this time... this will be on my terms or not at all."*

Of course she was getting a little ahead of herself as there really was no relationship to speak of at that point; simply an abundance of mutual admiration and the revelation by both of them that their interest in one another was most assuredly more than platonic and most definitely physical.

But nonetheless, time would tell. She couldn't help but wonder and hope that Mike was the one. She was counting on it; after all, he appeared to be everything she wanted in a man; handsome, educated, sincere, impeccably dressed and at least thus far; considerate.

Provided he didn't turn out to be a secret serial killer or weekend pornographer with a bigger shoe fetish than her, she was quite content to consider him a perfect fit.

Chapter 5

The next morning as Evie got dressed for work she wondered how the day would go. She knew they had the account wrapped up and Luzon would be in that morning to sign the papers but her mind was on that magic moment she shared with Mike the night before; little else mattered anymore.

It was so perfect she thought; gazing into each other's eyes and then their lips meeting for the most perfect and beautiful kiss she had ever experienced. She could still imagine his lips pressed against hers and she longed to feel that sensation once again.

She also wondered what Mike was thinking. Would he still be interested? Was he perhaps upset that they didn't consummate their relationship the evening before? Or was he just being smooth and playing a game designed for one purpose; to make her his most highly coveted conquest to date.

But all the thoughts in her head had to wait; she had to get to work…and to Mike. She actually felt nervous for the first time in years as she fumbled with blouse after blouse; blue, white, lace embroidery, big buttons small buttons, high collar, low collar; she had them all and tried on just about every one that went with the skirt she had on while parading back and forth in front of the mirror practicing what she might say when she saw Mike along with a dozen different poses and expressions.

After an hour she had accumulated a pile of clothes on her bed that rivaled the size of the Washington Monument but still hadn't found the right top. She gave up and just buttoned up the one she had on in a huff and left.

She wasn't at all happy with her selection but she was running late and would have to live with it for the moment. But of course, if worse came to worse she could always go out on her lunch hour and buy another blouse and change at work…and if things didn't go right with Mike she'd be in dire need of some 'retail therapy' anyway so it would be a good excuse to shop either way.

She arrived at her office fifteen minutes later than usual and slid into her big leather chair behind her desk as Gail came trotting in with her morning coffee.

"*Thank you Gail*" Evie said with an unusually cheerful tone of voice for that time of morning but quickly caught herself and corrected her tone.

Gail put the coffee down; *"The Luzon meeting is at nine in Ballantine's office."*

She acknowledged with a businesslike *"Excellent Gail, thank you!"*

Then Gail said *"Wait a minute...are you ok?"*

Evie replied; *"Yes of course I am."*

"No you're not"

"Ah, yes I am Gail"

"No you're not...you're better than ok!"

"And what prey tell is that supposed to mean?"

"You're feeling wonderful this morning; something is different."

To offset Gail's razor sharp female love detection radar Evie quipped *"Gee, I wasn't aware I've been so miserable on a consistent basis in the mornings Gail"*

"Oh I didn't mean it that way and you know it!" Gail snapped half kidding and half annoyed at her comment.

"I'm just pulling your leg Gail; I guess I'm just happy about snagging the Luzon account"

"I heard... nice going boss...but mmmm...that isn't it... It's something else; oh my god; your eyes are sparkling and you're a little flushed; you're glowing and that can only mean one thing; you've met someone haven't you!"

"I meet a lot of people Gail" she said in between sips of her coffee trying desperately to remain professional and keep from screaming *I'm crazy about Mike!* at the top of her lungs to everyone in the office and the people below on the street and briefly even considered throwing a ticker tape parade to mark the event to alert the good citizens of Gotham.

Despite her cool demeanor and inner turmoil Evie was bursting to tell Gail about the moment she shared with Mike but just couldn't do it. She needed to remain professional and detached; and plus she was so tired from talking about it with her friends on the phone all night until the wee hours she was all talked out by that point.

"Ok boss…If you say there's nothing going on then I guess there's nothing going on" Gail said with a tone that clearly indicated she didn't buy into Evie's half-hearted attempt at creating a diversion.

Evie replied laughing *"Are we resorting to reverse psychology now? Drop it Gail, I mean it!"* as she sorted through her messages as if nothing was going on.

An hour later she was in Mr. Ballantine's office making small talk waiting for Luzon and Mike to arrive so they could finalize the deal. Luckily Ballantine's secretary announced their arrival moments later and showed them in. Evie could barely concentrate on what Ballantine was saying and hoped he hadn't noticed just how hopelessly lost in wonderland she was.

She tried in vain not to even look at Mike but every few minutes their eyes would meet and they would both twitch slightly as if being jolted by a low voltage shock and avert their gaze as not to alert anyone to the invisible sparks of electricity that filled the room.

Luzon was well aware of what was going on and smiled at the sight of the young would-be lovers struggling to remain focused and professional yet doing such a painfully horrific job of it.

All the while Evie was simply replaying the previous evening's events over and over in her head. Her thoughts were racing; on the one hand she was glad her and Mike hadn't taken things a step further the night before or things would have unbelievably awkward that morning.

On the other hand she considered the fact that things were already hopelessly complicated and awkward between them even though they hadn't given into temptation and slept together so there really wasn't much she could do under the circumstances except try to get Mike alone and gauge his reaction. How could it make things any worse?

Mike was off in space thinking much the same thing but they both managed to get through the meeting somehow and at the end of it Luzon formally signed on. It was official; contractual; Eve and Mike would be handling the campaign together. That was exactly what she had hoped for.

Luzon took Evie and Mike aside after the meeting and said in a whisper so no one else would hear;

"If you two kids take even a small portion of the passion you obviously have for each other and apply it to this campaign it's going to be a huge success...don't disappoint me!"

He smiled, winked and sauntered off.

Both Evie and Mike stood there shocked for a moment unable to understand how Luzon was able to see what was going on between them so easily; was it that obvious or was Luzon perhaps far more perceptive than they had anticipated or were they just really bad actors?

Whatever the case, they both stood there next to each other just looking around the room trying to avoid locking eyes and after a minute or so just walked off to their respective offices leaving an uncomfortable silence behind in Ballantine's office.

Once back in her office Eve paced back and forth, fidgeted with her pen for a few moments and then decided to call Mike to come to her office so they could talk. As she began to dial she heard someone clearing their throat and looked up. It was him.

"Hey beautiful! You look a little distracted...anything I can do to help?" he said while leaning against her doorframe with his hands in his pockets looking like a matinee idol from the forties. All he needed was a fedora to complete the look.

She almost jumped out of her skin as she didn't expect to see him standing there. She wasn't ready; they were both extremely nervous but tried in vain to pretend they weren't.

"Well, that went well don't you think?" (Mike)

"Yes, it did, very productive....yes...it went very well" (Evie)

"Yes, very well" (Mike)

"Uh huh!" (Evie)

"Much better than I anticipated" (Mike)

"Me too" (Evie)

"Good work by the way" (Mike)

"Thank you...same to you" (Evie)

"Stellar job!" (Mike)

They had no idea what they were saying. They were locked into each other's eyes and moving closer with every nonsensical word they spoke until they were inches from each other.

"Well, here we are" (Mike)

"Yes it appears so" (Evie)

They couldn't resist anymore; they had run out of silly superficial banter and couldn't deny their passion for one moment longer. They began kissing like two love struck teenagers right there in Evie's office with their arms wrapped tightly around each other exploring every soft curve and tense muscle while their tongues danced together to the rhythm of their pounding hearts.

"Stop Mike!" she said gasping for air and pushing his hand down in the midst of it eagerly trying to pull up her skirt.

"Ok, sorry!"

"We can't do this here, this isn't the time or place" she exclaimed while making a fanning motion with her hand to dissipate the heat.

"You're right....how about the stairwell in five minutes?"

Evie laughed *"That's not what I meant silly!...and by the way; stairwell?....ewww!!"*

Mike looked deep into her eyes with a half-smile, leaned towards her and said *"I know... I was just trying to lighten the mood...sorry...bad attempt at humor at the wrong time..."*

Evie looked relieved.

He tried again;

"Ok...how about this...we meet by the elevators at one o'clock and go for lunch and talk this out before things go any further."

"Agreed! I think it's the rational thing to do under the circumstances?" she said rummaging through her bag nervously with hands shaking while trying desperately

to maintain her composure and find a cigarette that she knew perfectly well she wouldn't be able to smoke unless she went outside essentially rendering the entire exercise completely futile.

Then she took out a tissue and signaled Mike;

"Come here you silly boy... you've got lipstick all over your face" and proceeded to wipe it off.

"Thanks Eve...damn...is it on my collar too?"

"No...and what do you care? Do you have a secret wife at home that will be checking?"

"Hardly...but I would look pretty silly walking around with lipstick on my collar"

"I guess you're right, that would look silly...OK, you're good to go. Now get out of here before I say yes to the stairwell."

Mike walked out past Gail who appeared suddenly at the door. He didn't seem at all perturbed by her sudden and somewhat masterful materialization and gave her a playful wink as he glided out into the hallway past her humming.

Neither of the lovebirds realized that she had been standing at the doorway almost the entire time watching the whole awkward yet sexually charged encounter.

"Oh my god Evie; it's Mike! You and Mike!" Gail gasped almost as if in horror walking back and forth with her hand covering her mouth as if the end of the world had

just been announced on the news and alien space crafts were landing on Staten Island at that very moment.

"Oh Evie, be careful! Sweetie, that guy is trouble...he's going to break your heart believe me!"

Evie was a little annoyed at Gail's comments and said with a rather perfunctory tone of voice while fumbling to adjust her skirt and blouse while looking down at the papers on her desk and then casually walking over to the mirror on the wall to check her makeup;

"We're not having this discussion; and not a word about this to anyone, are we clear?"

"Perfectly!"

"That will be all Gail"

Gail was genuinely concerned for Evie. She had been her assistant for five years so she had grown somewhat close to her at least professionally. Evie on the other hand had always made an effort to keep Gail at an arm's length and not engage in personal discussions with her.

Eve was acutely aware of what gossip mongers the majority of the assistants were especially when they had any details about their bosses to sling around during their lunch breaks; and until that moment they never had anything on Eve.

But nonetheless Evie was undaunted by Gail's negative reaction. She just assumed Gail was wrong or jealous as she really didn't know Mike the way she did. After all

Evie had been working closely with him for the past two years and he had always been a perfect gentleman. So what would Gail know about it? She's just an assistant she thought to herself.

Evie quickly recognized that her thoughts towards her loyal assistant were demeaning and uncalled for but she was prepared to rationalize her relationship with Mike in any way necessary at that point.

She had fallen further and harder than even she realized; that pivotal point where the brain stops thinking and the heart begins to impose its iron will regardless of circumstance, facts, or the possible disastrous consequences.

It seemed like an eternity but one o'clock finally came. Evie grabbed her coat and darted past Gail "*I'm going for lunch; back in an hour or so.*"

She didn't want to have to endure any more of Gail's interrogation tactics so she sailed past Gail with the intensity, deliberation and speed of a runner crossing the finish line at the New York Marathon.

This of course only served to confirm Gail's suspicions about the nature of Evie's urgent appointment and the status of her relationship with Mike; Gail also looked forward to lunch that day.

Mike intercepted Evie at the elevator; "*Hey, goin' my way?*"

"*Shush...someone might hear you!*" she whispered with eyes darting back and forth suspiciously scanning the hall.

He whispered back "*Did you bring the package?*"

"*What package?*"

"*I don't know...you're acting like we're on a secret mission or something so I figured there must be a mysterious package involved and possibly even a code word.*"

She gave him the evil eye for the first time and said "*yeah, I've got a code word for ya buddy!*"...he just chuckled and didn't ask what it was...perhaps it was self-explanatory.

They stepped into the crowded elevator; "*Oh my gosh, I didn't see you there, how are you?*" She said to Mike acting as if they hardly knew one another as if no one had noticed that they just got on the elevator together a second earlier.

Mike decided to have a little fun and play along.

"*I'm fine; thank you...Evie is it?*"

"Yes Mick"

"Mike!"

"*Pardon?*"

"*Mike, my name is Mike*"

"*And so it is*"

Mike decided to 'up the ante' as they took up a position next to each other at the rear of the elevator after a few people got out at the next stop;

"How's Alphonse your boyfriend? I heard he finally got over the venereal disease and the rash is gone..."

"Thanks for asking Mick! He's JUST great, (she jerks and almost shouts out certain words as Mike discretely delivers a series of gentle playful fanny squeezes in the rear of the crowded elevator to throw her off her game)

But she continued nonetheless as did the fanny squeezes;

"... and say Mick how's your WIFE Trixie? Did the electroshock therapy HELP her psychotic and paranoid delusions?"

"Absolutely Jane"

"Evie!"

"What?"

"The name is Evie"

"Right...and so it is....anyway, Trixie is going to be staying at Shady Oaks for a little longer than anticipated but should be released after the prefrontal lobotomy next year and after she gives birth to the psychiatrists illegitimate child "

"Oh that's wonderful...at least she won't have to work that street corner anymore!"

By that point they could barely contain there laughter as they played their fun new game for the now eager ears of the anonymous passengers on the elevator.

But then Mike's gentle playful squeezes suddenly became slower and increasingly sensual as he ran his hand along the curvature of Evie's fanny and squeezed ever so gently over the tight soft material of her skirt.

She began to sigh softly as her hand discretely grasped the back of Mike's suit jacket clenching her fist with each stroke of his hand as it caressed her while she trembled with sexual energy. Neither could speak from that point forward.

DING! Lobby.

"Getting a little too hot for ya Mikey?" Evie kidded once they made it out onto the sidewalk and into the welcoming arms of a refreshing cool breeze that rushed down the avenue like a wave at high tide washing away the last remaining vestiges of summer and discretely signaling the arrival of the brisk and colorful fall that lay ahead.

Evie pulled out a beautifully embroidered handkerchief from her bag and gently dabbed at the tiny beads of perspiration rolling down Mike's forehead as he stood facing the wind with his nose up like a dog sticking its head out of a car window enjoying the breeze.

"Can ya blame me?" he said still somewhat worked up and a little embarrassed.

Evie put one hand on her hip and said "*Sweetie, I'm a woman; I can figure out a way to blame a man for just about anything* (she chuckled) *but I ought to slap you for grabbing my fanny like that in the elevator you naughty boy!*"

"*How about a kiss instead Jane?*"

She didn't retort but instead grabbed the lapels of his jacket and pulled him towards her for some of the most sensual kissing that had probably ever taken place on that particular stretch of sidewalk.

After they had finished a woman of sixty-ish that caught their act in the elevator stopped for a moment on her way past the two lovebirds and muttered '*You two should be ashamed of yourselves…* (turning to Mike) *…cavorting with this trollop with your wife so ill and all*"

She trotted off with a 'humph" and her nose in the air apparently ready to battle the forces of evil on the next block.

Evie looked at Mike in horror; "*Oh my God! Trollop? Wow...who uses that word anymore?*"

They both started laughing as they walked off hand in hand to the restaurant hoping they wouldn't be accosted again by *Super Senior*.

Chapter 6

Friday night came quickly. It was their first official date. Evie had picked up a bottle of wine and a French loaf as a house warming gift, jumped in a cab and was on her way over to Mike's for the very first time.

On the way there she suddenly realized that Mike had been living there for some time and as such had no idea why she was bringing a house warming present....the house was already warm...and would no doubt heat up considerably during the course of the evening she cogitated with a sense of exhilaration.

Obviously she wasn't thinking clearly but was quite enjoying the feeling of being love drunk. She gave the French loaf to the cabbie and opted to just bring along the wine.

Mike lived in an upscale building just off Fifth Avenue. It was one of those buildings that utterly reeked of money as well as political and corporate clout.

"Holy shit!" she whispered to herself with a lump in her throat as she stood there on the sidewalk looking up at the enormous imposing building like Alice in Wonderland.

The doorman noticed her immediately and opened the massive glass door with a warm disarming smile as if to say *"don't worry child, come on in, no one's going to hurt you, it's ok"* obviously quite aware of her trepidation.

For a moment or so she couldn't even move…it was as if her feet suddenly weighed a couple of hundred pounds apiece and were glued to the sidewalk but she broke free after a few seconds and tried her best to act as if she belonged there while discretely taking deep breaths to keep calm.

"Thank you" Evie said with a big toothy grin as she strode past the doorman through the open door like a movie star that had just stepped out of a limousine and was seeking refuge in the exclusive building from the mob of adoring fans and paparazzi crowding the sidewalk.

As she turned her head back for one final glance at her imaginary adoring public she walked straight into the inner glass door and bounced off it like a tennis ball tumbling to the ground; game, set, match!

Not even a second later she was hoisted effortlessly to her feet by two extremely strong arms from behind. It was the doorman;

"Are you ok?"

"Yes I think so...thank you" she said while fighting back the tears of embarrassment and brushing herself off; not that those imported marble floor tiles she was just laying on were ever allowed to get dirty.

"Don't worry Miss Evie; you'd be surprised how many people do that...did it once myself the first week I worked here...name's Edward by the way" as he extended his enormous hand which dwarfed hers when they shook.

"How do you know my name?"

"I'm telepathic...it's a gift" he said with a near perfect poker face on.

She stared at him for a moment evaluating his comment trying to decide whether he was joking or perhaps slightly insane but his budding smile gave it away before Evie could experience her second moment of extreme imbecility since arriving approximately ninety seconds earlier.

He immediately continued *"...just kidding, actually Mr. Dubrow told us to expect an incredibly beautiful woman at about this time that just happens to fit your description"*

"How sweet of you to say! Thank you!" she said.

This was yet another one of those awkward moments in her life where someone had commented on her beauty and it made her even more uncomfortable than usual given the fact that she had just been picked up off the floor after walking into a glass door like a complete ditz...that type of thing never makes one feel like a Mensa member.

If anything she was relieved that Edward wasn't telepathic...the thoughts in her head about what might take place later in the evening with Mike would have definitely qualified as her third and crowning moment of imbecility....well above the national average and Mensa's idiocy quotient; and probably a record for that particular building.

She momentarily perceived the comment regarding her beauty as a backhanded compliment particularly because of what had just happened and assumed the doorman was now simply placating her and in all likelihood thought she was just another one of Mikes bimbo's...which in reality wasn't the case at all.

The doorman, like everyone else Eve had ever met was sincerely taken aback by her striking beauty and in reality hadn't made any judgments whatsoever regarding her level of intelligence or talent or anything else for that matter.

As always, such notions and assumptions were all figments of Evie's own imagination and nothing more. Those that have been blessed with a high powered imagination and exceptional creative ability are fortunate indeed but on occasion it tends to bite them on the ass without warning.

But regardless of what was going on in her head Evie was a master of concealing her completely unfounded feelings of inadequacy and quickly brushed away any further thoughts of such things and carried on.

"I feel so darn silly...I don't usually walk into doors like a complete idiot"

"You didn't walk into that door like an idiot Miss Evie; you walked into that door like a graceful young lady that just happened to be looking in the opposite direction her body was traveling in at the time of impact; physics along with Murphy's Law produced a less than favorable result unfortunately; the main thing is that you are ok!"

He winked, smiled and they shared a heartfelt laugh over the now seemingly inconsequential incident.

Newly invigorated Evie continued on without further incident to the inner sanctum of the building and wondered why such an intelligent and articulate man was working as a mere doorman.

"Ho-ly- ssshhit!" She whispered to herself as she entered the grand lobby all the while texting Susan and Lena *"U should c this place; wow; fancy schmancy; like something out of a movie....sooo nervous I could die"*

Symphony music played softly over the loudspeakers as the clicking of her high heels reverberated throughout the lobby with every step during her long agonizing walk to the concierge desk.

It was like a hotel she thought. And she was right; it was once a hotel and had been converted into condominiums about twenty years prior but it still felt and for the most part, by design, looked like a hotel.

Evie's building, although relatively expensive by most people's standards, Tom's for example; and befitting the lifestyles of the young professionals that lived there, paled in comparison.

It was just an old industrial building that was converted to condominium lofts years earlier; no overqualified witty doorman and no massive glass wood framed doors to bounce off of like an idiot during a movie star fantasy.

She had seen buildings like this while browsing through real estate magazines at the spa but never knew anyone that actually lived in one. And now there she was; it was like a dream come true.

She approached the huge mahogany concierge desk cautiously almost expecting the security staff to be huddled behind it laughing while watching the replay footage of her slamming into the front door on the monitor and taking bets on the next object she would collide with before leaving.

But no such thing occurred.

Her apprehension and anxiety were immediately alleviated upon her arrival at the desk.

"You must be Evelyn" the distinguished looking older man said with a warm gracious smile.

"Yes"

"Welcome to the Winchester; Mr. Dubrow has been expecting you, please sign in"

After signing the guest register the gentleman at the desk said *"Have a wonderful evening Miss Evelyn... Penthouse"* as he motioned to the elevators to his right as if he was presenting 'door number three' on a game show; which was oddly appropriate as she felt like a contestant on a fictional reality show called Dating Mikey!

The elevator doors opened and she gasped slightly...and of course the texting started again immediately with brief interludes to snap multiple pictures of the massive elevator with her cell phone camera.

In fact the elevators in this building could pass for the bachelor suites in her building; they were huge and even had seats in them. She felt more than a little overwhelmed at that point as "OMG" text messages flooded in from all her girlfriends. Apparently they were all quite impressed and intrigued with her foray into the lap of luxury.

She fully expected Mike to live in an upscale building but she couldn't understand how he could possibly afford something like this; she knew what his income was and this building was well out of his league.... impossibly so.

And her thoughts were well founded as a smaller suite in that building, even if you happened to be on the official 'whose who' shortlist of New York's elite and were worthy of being considered as a possible resident by the board, would cost well over eight million dollars with a handsome six figure annual property tax bill to boot.

She sat on the bench nervously touching up her lipstick as the elevator silently whisked her up to the penthouse level with the velocity of a space shuttle but none of the noise or vibration.

Her knees felt like cottage cheese when she got up to face the doors in anticipation of her lunar landing on Mars;

The door silently slid open.

"Hey beautiful! We meet again!" Mike said standing there with arms outstretched; *"Welcome to my humble abode!"*

Eve just stood there paralyzed for a moment; she felt totally out of her element again; just like she did when she arrived in New York and stepped off the bus for the first time and was totally overwhelmed by what she saw.

Her feet simply wouldn't move as she stood there with an expression on her face that had 'help me' written all over it.

"What's wrong?" Mike said smiling, intentionally trying to ease her obvious debilitating case of nerves; *"Are you ok my dear?"*

Evie just said *"I'm sorry I've never been in a place like this before so I'm a little overwhelmed...I've seen it a million times passing by on the street or in a cab and often wondered what it was like inside and now that I'm here it's a little much, I'm sorry"*

"Geeez Evie is that all? I was afraid it was something serious."

He laughed and continued; *"It's just a stuffy old building that happens to be in a ridiculously overpriced neighborhood...nothing to be intimidated about here"*

"It's so beautiful" she cooed.

"Well, if you care to come out of there I'd be happy to show you the rest of it" he said while chuckling with hand outstretched as if coaxing an infant to take their first step.

Apparently she had completely forgotten that she was still inside the elevator.

"Oh my god, I'm sorry" she said as she cautiously stepped out taking his hand and then freezing again as if waiting to be frisked by security before being allowed to continue any further down the hall.

"Well this is definitely a first"

"What do you mean?"

"I don't think I've ever heard you say the word 'sorry' before; kind of refreshing actually!" Mike said in jest.

"Very funny Mick!"

"Ah yes, she's back ladies and gentlemen! And hey I've got a great idea; instead of spending the evening here

by the elevator why don't we throw caution to the wind and actually go further into my suite for a drink and dinner? The view is much nicer...just a thought."

"You mean this is actually the inside of your suite?...the elevator opens directly into your suite?"

"It would appear so yes"

They both laughed; Evie regained the use of her legs once again and off they went.

When Eve stepped out *"Oh- my- God!"* were the only words she could muster for a moment or two as she just stood there gawking at the en-suite vestibule that was in reality larger than her entire apartment.

Once they reached the living room her ability to engage in superficial banter once again eluded her and *"How in God's name can you afford this?"* just fell out of her mouth.

It was as ill-timed and inappropriate as putting a match to ones bum and farting during an elegant dinner with high profile clients or one's in-laws...but there it was nonetheless.

Mike wasn't offended or put off in the least; he simply smiled and said in a matter of fact tone of voice; *"I can't!"*

"Then how did you..."

Mike cut her off and proceeded to explain as he led her from room to room;

"I can't afford this any more than you can my dear. My parents own it and they graciously allow me to live here. Like you I'm just a humble young advertising executive working far too hard for far too little money... but seriously speaking, yes I do realize that I am very fortunate in case you were wondering where my thinking and ego stack up on the reality scale. I don't know, what can say; I was born into money; we've always had plenty of it and I fully admit that I haven't a clue how it feels to be poor or have to struggle financially."

She oohed and ahhhed as they moved from room to room to his humble rambling and at times almost nonsensical narrative delivered with an awkwardness that unwittingly revealed a hint of guilt regarding his station in life which was as much a first for him as Evie's uncomfortable encounter with the word 'sorry' moments earlier.

Nonetheless he continued with his rambling soliloquy;

"My folks paid for my education but I do realize there are kids out there that actually have to pay their own way and eat mac and cheese every night...which I actually do myself, more than I'd like to admit; it's one of my favorite sinful socially unacceptable meal choices; (opening one of the doors to the pantry which contained at least a couple of dozen boxes of it)*...but the point is I didn't have to scrimp. In fact I didn't have to do anything except get good grades and let the family accountant worry about who gets paid when and for what. I don't know how it feels to be hungry or how it feels to not even have change for the bus or how it feels to not own a car...let alone anything lesser than a*

Mercedes or Jaguar...never been in a Chevy actually"
making a yucky face at the mere thought of having to
endure such barbarism.

Evie just sat there in a state of shock and didn't even
comprehend most of what he had said. She was
flabbergasted as she had no idea he came from money...
at least not that kind of money....and the most dangerous
kind no less....OLD MONEY.

She tried desperately to speak but couldn't even come
up with anything stupid to say much less something
intelligent so she just sat there, her eyes scanning the
room trying to process what was happening.

Mike could plainly see that she was having considerable
difficulty with it all so he did what he did best; kept
talking;

*I haven't a clue how the 'other half' lives...I admit
it but listen, that doesn't make me a shitty person; I
realize how fortunate I am...I don't have to work...I
could just take a cushy job from my father and basically
do nothing for the rest of my life or pretend to give a
damn like your client Rena does while riding on the coat
tails of what someone else had built; but I don't. I live
here because it's convenient...my parents don't want
to rent to strangers so the arrangement works well; I
pay the maintenance fees so I feel like I'm contributing
something and not sponging....and you know what?...I
like my job and I like to work...but you know what I
hate the most?*

"What?"

"Rambling on and on about money and all these material trappings; and that my dear is precisely why I don't bring my dates up here..."

Evie suddenly found her voice and was somewhat functional again;

"Come on now Casanova, I'm sure you've had dozens of girls up here."

"No mam! Not a single one...aside from my mom and my sister, and a couple of female cousins that drop by on occasion; but other than that you have the distinction of being the first (he put his hand up in the stop position and tilted his head forward) *hang on...that didn't come out right...it sounds arrogant and patronizing ...as if I'm doing you a favor or something and I didn't mean it like that at all...let me rephrase"*

He paused for a moment taking a deep breath with head tilted back and then started over. For the first time in his life he was actually at somewhat of a loss for words; but he made a sincerely valiant effort:

"See?...this....this right here...this is what I'm talking about...I can talk my way in and out of sales meetings and campaign brainstorming sessions with the greatest of ease and sell just about anything to anyone but having you here with me tonight means so much to me I can barely manage a coherent sentence and am rambling incessantly...that's what you do to me!"

"Well I suppose it's only fair that I show you what you do to me as well then"

Evie cupped his face with her hands, pulled him close, kissed him gently on the lips and whispered *"that was the sweetest thing anyone has ever said to me...thank you"* and they continued to kiss.

But then something odd happened after the kissing had subsided; as Mike continued to speak about something, Evie's imagination overpowered her thoughts as it often did at the most inopportune moments and she went into one of her daydreams and thought to herself;

"oh my god...imagine if I was with Tom right now and not here in this beautiful penthouse with Mike; we'd be huddled like prisoners on some ghastly smelly sofa eating off TV trays watching some silly hockey game in some little hovel in the Bronx or Queens or somewhere equally as horrid; if only he could see me right now; sewer worker; what a joke"

She excused herself to go and freshen up in hopes of eluding the thoughts of Tom. But as she washed her hands and touched up her makeup there in the bathroom the intrusive thoughts simply continued unabated;

"yeah... sitting around the kitchen table on a Saturday morning clipping coupons before going grocery shopping in our pickup truck wearing our sensible middle class shoes...and perhaps there would be children...OH MY GOD! Children...that's just horrible...I can just see Tom in the kitchen holding our baby with those big hairy gorilla arms of his in tight jeans and a tight t-shirt....oh my god what am I thinking.....stop it stop it stop it...Mike is perfect and so sweet and we could have the perfect life together...we will have the perfect life together!!"

Mike interjected with a knock on the bathroom door;

"Are you ok in there?"

"I'll be right out" she sang; more than likely a compensatory measure; no one is ever that cheery when they're in the bathroom.

When she came out they retired to the living room as Mike proceeded to pour her a glass of imported French Champagne at a price of over $500.00 per bottle; all but forgetting that Eve had brought her own bottle for the occasion…or more likely conveniently setting it aside as if it would be tantamount to drinking motor oil.

Evie took a sip; *"mmmm….this is very good….*so *how do you feel about kids?"*

He didn't miss a beat and totally unaffected by her surprising question said *"No interest at all I'm afraid"*

"Thank God. Same here!" said Evie with the same trite emotionally flat tone of voice that Mike had just employed.

"Well that was an interesting question Eve, any particular reason?"

"Nope…just curious…..it's a girl thing!"

"Ok…so how about we drink this stuff; it's a guy thing! Cheers!"

"Cheers Mick!" Evie said raising her glass as if to declare victory for no apparent reason other than an excuse to ingest the glass of alcohol as quickly as possible.

Oddly enough she had the same defeated look in her eyes Tom did that day he ran into her outside Angelino's and she rejected his proposal to go to Susan's party.

But aside from the intrusive daydreams and thoughts of terrible Tom the sewer guy, Evie and Mike enjoyed what turned out to be an extraordinarily wonderful evening.

They stood out on the terrace, sipped their perfectly chilled Champagne and gazed out over the Manhattan skyline; one bottle, two bottles and counting after an hour or so in the crisp night air.

Evie felt more like a princess in a fairy tale with each passing sip and glance into her would-be Prince Charming's sparkling baby blue eyes.

She couldn't believe that she was actually standing there with this incredibly good looking intelligent young man that apparently was falling for her as fast and hard as she was for him. It was heaven; a moment she would never forget as long as she lived she told herself.

Her head was swirling slightly from the champagne and she felt like she was floating on air. He stepped closer and brushed away the hair from her face and kissed her softly.

She was now officially defenseless; a blubbering heap of jelly…a de-clawed feline meowing and purring softly at the magical touch of the one who owns her heart; she couldn't stop his advances if she wanted to; and she wanted him, all of him; body and soul.

She had hoped Mike had forgotten all about their 'no sex' rule and longed for the brash rogue she had heard so much about from the girls at work to emerge like an untamed savage and ravage her from head to her pretty little pedicured toes.

They kissed passionately in the cool night air rarely coming up for air apparently enjoying every second of their gentle sexually charged embrace. But despite the perfection of the moment Mike suddenly put the brakes on;

"Evie, what say we order some dinner and continue this afterwards?"

"I thought you were going to cook for me?"

"I got tied up with a business call and burned the sauce...sorry"

But she didn't care about that. She was more concerned about the fact that he apparently wasn't catching her 'take me now' signals and was somewhat miffed by his acute case of romantic ineptitude-itis.

But commonsense prevailed and she quickly realized that Mike was actually taking her seriously and was simply adhering to her wishes...which she really didn't expect him to but how would he know that? He's just a guy she thought...what does he really know about women?

But make no mistake; The Maestro saw the signals and could feel her eagerness through her tongue as they kissed; she was ready to make love to him regardless of the silly rule they had agreed upon; but as utterly agonizing as it was trying to keep the party that was going on in his pants a secret he gave her his word and wasn't going to breach their agreement.

"Phew...I better slowdown with this champagne before I get too silly" Eve said.

"Well, we wouldn't want that now would we my dear" Mike replied jokingly well aware that she was moving perhaps a little too voraciously with regard to her alcohol consumption.

As convenient as it would have been for him to pounce and later blame the alcohol, he was acutely aware that she wasn't one of his playmates and as such didn't intend to treat her like one or create the need for bad excuses to mollify bad behavior.

He was truly falling for her and saw her as an equal both professionally and personally; unfamiliar territory indeed.

She was far and above any girl he had dated previously; that unique combination of brains and beauty that most men can't recognize and appreciate let alone ever possess. And make no mistake he wanted to possess her just as she wanted him; body and soul.

Dinner was impeccable. She ordered salad and the French onion soup. He had a cheeseburger, fries and onion rings with a chocolate milkshake.

"So what's with the burger Mick? I thought you rich people only ate foods that no one else can pronounce"

"Well Jane, to me this is a delicacy...good honest American fare."

"You can't be serious Horatio"

"I'm quite serious Griselda; when I was growing up we always had formal dinners served by our house staff and us kids never ate regular food like pizza, fries and cheeseburgers because it was considered not only unhealthy but uncivilized. My parents considered it food for the common masses. But I never bought into that crap; I thought it was just pure snobbery so one day I went to a fast food restaurant and decided to see why the majority of the population loves the stuff so much; one bite and it was pretty obvious; it tasted wonderful; so I've been eating it ever since; not all the time of course as I know it's not the healthiest choice but every now and again as a sinful treat."

"You're an interesting guy Bartholomew"

"Bartholomew?   (He laughed) *Wow, that's stretching the pet names a bit isn't it?"*

"Well Griselda isn't exactly flattering"

"Touché miss Jane!"

"Much better!"

They chuckled and were clearly both quite relaxed and enjoying each other's company and verbal horseplay immensely. It had become 'their thing'; a private little game that no one else knew about...except for all of Eve's girlfriends…they of course thought it was unbelievably romantic and 'cute' as they put it.

After dinner they retired to the entertainment room; a huge space with twelve foot high ceilings, floor to ceiling windows flanked by enormous drapes tied back with velvet ropes to provide a spectacular view of the city skyline and a massive TV screen of biblical proportions that descended as if from the heavens to cover one entire wall with a click of a button on a remote that had so many buttons it looked like a control panel from the space shuttle; most definitely every man's idea of heaven.

They kicked off their shoes and hopped up onto one of three large sofas like a couple of school kids at a pajama party giggling and laughing;

"You know, I had you pictured so differently Mikey… and you've got some mustard on your lip by the way" Evie said as she sipped yet another glass of champagne while enjoying her après dinner ciggy.

Mike lit a cigarette, rubbed the mustard off his lip and said *"Different how? You mean good different or bad different?"*

"Not sure yet; just different"

"Ah yes, the complicated mind of the female, ladies and gentlemen…a guy never really knows what goes on in there"

"No sir, but in all fairness, you're doing pretty well so far according to my checklist" She said laughingly while making a checking motion with her cigarette.

"I'll do my best"

"You do of course realize you're fighting a bit of an uphill battle; despite your obviously good intentions, you do have quite a reputation as a playboy of sorts; the kind of guy that isn't even looking for love; just physical romance as often as possible with as many women as possible. The kind of guy that has no intention of ever settling down with one woman; I just can't play that game. So tell me Mikey, am I just another potential conquest or is there more to this wonderful evening of ours?"

"Wow, nothing like being blunt huh? (He laughed) *But I do understand where you're coming from."*

"And where exactly is that Maestro?"

"So you know about that little nickname huh?"

"Oh I've heard plenty mister"

"Ok, ok (he laughed) *it's all true; guilty as charged. I've dated more than my fair share of women and for the most part yes, it's been purely physical"*

"Well that's comforting" Evie said half-jokingly and half sarcastically.

Mike gently took her hand and put aside the joking for the moment;

"Evie, think about it for a minute; how on earth is a guy supposed to find the right girl if he doesn't date any, or so few that he'd be a hundred years old before he finds one he really clicks with?"

"Boy, I really do hate it when you're right..."

"Thank you...I think. But look; people blow things way out of proportion; yes, I only date women I'm physically attracted to; I mean why would I date women that I find physically repulsive? I mean would you date a guy you find physically unappealing?"

"Ok, you're still right and I still hate you" She said with squinted eyes as Mike continued;

"And yes, of course nature takes it course, why wouldn't it? Those girls were all perfectly willing, and some quite insistent I might add, to ruffle the bed sheets; completely consensual"

"I bet"

"I'm trying to be serious and sincere here Eve"

"Sorry"

"Anyway, after a few dates it would always become apparent to me that there was really nothing of any substance going on aside from the sex; like a great appetizer or desert but with no substantial main course in between that leaves you temporarily satisfied but ultimately still hungry"

"Nice analogy Mick"

"Thank you, so glad you liked it but seriously, that's why I would discontinue the relationships; not because I was 'done' with them and couldn't wait to select something else from the menu but because there was simply no good reason to continue. So does that make me a monster?"

"Appetizer...hmmm... nice touch maestro but I guess the answer to the monster question depends on where I appear on this menu of yours"

There was a full minute of silence as the two of them searched each other eyes for answers before Evie broke the silence;

"Well well well, the silver tongued devil himself is at a loss for words. What, no answer there mister maestro?" she said all the while taking his silence as a sign of rejection or avoidance and thinking about getting her coat and leaving.

But then she got her answer; and there was no misinterpreting it;

"I'm falling in love with you Evie...there is no menu; just you!"

"Yeah, that's a good answer alright"

"Well you asked for it...I hope it..."

"Just shut up and kiss me while you're ahead on points Ricardo!"

And kiss they did; passionately and for several minutes at which time Mike said;

"Evie....we have to stop!"

"Why?"

"The no sex rule, remember?"

Evie undid his tie, pulled it from underneath his collar and threw it on the floor;

"Never heard of it!"

They retired to the bedroom leaving a trail of clothing behind in case a search party would have to be called in incase they didn't make it out again.

Chapter 7

"Prepare to be crushed!" Sebastian shouted as he prepared himself for another rally in the squash court at the exclusive Reinhold Club in Yonkers.

He and Mike met there every Thursday evening at six pm sharp to slice away the week's frustration over a game of high intensity racquetball and drinks afterwards.

After an hour or so Sebastian's declaration came to fruition; he had handily won each game by a sizeable margin; more than usual. Mike was obviously preoccupied.

After showering and dressing they retired to the cigar lounge in the west wing of the building. This room was like something out of a movie; grand in scale and its masculine design with dark hardwood wide-plank floors as old as the structure itself, big leather chairs set in groups of two or three to create intimate seating areas throughout the room under towering wooden built-in bookshelves filled with old books from every academic discipline, particularly law and economics donated over the years by various members.

The walls were covered with dark mahogany paneling and precisely twelve large tiffany lamps hung from the soaring twenty foot ceilings; one over each seating cluster all dwarfed by the gargantuan period stone fireplace that graced the east wall like a friendly giant presiding over a small village of well-dressed drunken idiots.

The club was originally a mansion owned by a prominent New York shipping magnate in the early 1900's. When his wife died he decided to convert the building into a private gentlemen's club; a place where his friends could meet for various recreational activities; mainly to drink outrageously expensive, and at the time illegal, liquor during the prohibition period, smoke fine cigars and grope the bevy of young curvaceous girls that served them in tight fitting uniforms, silk seamed stockings and high heeled shoes.

Eventually it officially became a 'members only' club. It was handed down to his son and in turn his grandson who still owned the building and could be seen there on any given night holding court, drinking imported Madeira wine and enjoying a Cuban cigar with friends. The cigar room was in fact his great grandfather's original study.

Membership to the club was not open to the public at large and they meant 'membership' in the purest sense of the word. You had to be a member of a certain family or be recommended by a member of one of those families in order to be considered as a candidate. Both Sebastian and Mike belonged to such families so their membership was fundamentally a birth right.

Each received their membership status when they turned twenty one with an elaborate ceremony held at the club hosted by their fathers who still frequented the club particularly during the warm summer months when the Polo matches were held on the expansive grounds.

All members of the club were men; most of whom were older gentlemen with ties to Wall Street, the medical profession, Judges, lawyers, a few politicians and for the most part businessmen.

No sewer workers; and no women aside from those working in the kitchen or serving were allowed to set foot on the property....particularly member's wives; this was sacred ground!

"Good evening Mr. Dubrow, Mr. Decaine...anything to drink?"

"Good evening Natasha; the usual please"

"Very good...can I get you something to eat?"

"I'm sorry (Sebastian said) *what was that?"*

"Food...the stuff you put in your mouth with a fork while you're eating; want any?" Mike retorted.

Sebastian snapped out of his brief daydream; *"Sorry, yes, Filet Mignon with baked potato and spinach, corn and pea's please"*

"And for you Mr. Dubrow?"

"Cheeseburger with onion rings please Natasha" Mike replied while Sebastian proceeded to proudly perform his extensive repertoire of 'yucky faces' which entailed pursing his lips among various other bodily contortions as he did on any occasion Mike would order 'common' food; the implication of course was that common food was the equivalent of toxic waste.

Nonetheless it always made the server girls laugh; not because it was actually funny; because they had all seen the routine a hundred times and finally discovered it was more fun to laugh *at* Sebastian for being an idiot and earn an enormous tip in the process for their efforts in making Sebastian believe he was the cat's meow when in reality they had something from the other end of the cat in mind.

"Thank you gentlemen...back in a snap with your drinks" Natasha chuckled as she turned and clicked off on her high heels and slender stems with menu's in hand and a big smile on her face; Sebastian always enjoyed watching her walking away.

"Nice legs!"

"Well thank you Sebastian you rascal, I didn't know you cared!" Mike said jokingly.

"Not you, you imbecile! I meant Natasha!"

"I'm hurt Sebastian; would you like them more if I shaved them?" Mike said sticking up his leg and tugging up his pant leg.

"Fuck off Michael!"

"What, I'm not good enough for you anymore?" he replied in a melodramatic tone in an obvious effort to embarrass his old friend.

Mike raised his voice even louder for full humiliation value;

"Just come right out and say it Sebastian Decaine; you're breaking up with me aren't you!" and then performed an obvious phony cry while dabbing his eyes with a handkerchief and fanning himself like a southern Belle to the cheers and laughter of those in the room and the server girls that watched from the bar area; all cooing over Mike and his extraordinary sense of humor.

Even Sebastian started to laugh.

Mike stood up and took a bow as the room erupted with applause. Yes of course everyone understood that it was a joke; Mike and Sebastian's reputation for debauchery with the ladies was already legendary at the club and this certainly wasn't the first time they had performed one of their impromptu dinner theatre skits to the delight of the room.

While the applause still abounded Sebastian looked over at mike and with a big smile on his face said *"You're an asshole Michael, do you know that?"*

"Yes, and thank you for reminding me Sebastian"

Soon the room went back to its usual quiet hum as Natasha delivered dinner.

"The girls and I all thought that was very funny Mr. Dubrow" she said in a sweet tone of voice as she set the plates on the table with a look in her eyes that screamed 'please for god sake ask me out on a date Michael'

Unfortunately he didn't. He never did. He just thanked her and she left disappointed once again just like every other week.

"Mmmm....tasty" Sebastian said while digging into his steak like he hadn't been fed for a week but coming up for air briefly; *"mmm...and speaking of tasty how's it going with the trollop?"*

Mike didn't like the word trollop, particularly when Sebastian used it in reference to Evie but he let it go that time because it was probably passive aggressive payback for the laughs he just got at his old friends expense.

"You're the second person to call her a trollop this month"

"No shit! Imagine that! But tell me, how are dear old mama and papa going to take the news; telling them soon I assume? I trust they will be thrilled?"

"You know something? I really hate when you do that."

"What?"

"That...that thing; that trite arrogant question thing while you do the thing with your mouth and eyebrows while you ask your stupid fucking questions; kind of

like the yucky food faces; just come out and say it; you hate Evie and you think mom and dad will hate her as well"

"I don't hate her Michael and I do concede that she is breathtakingly beautiful and quite smart; but that's not the issue; the issue my misguided friend is that we have an obligation to our families to marry someone from our own social circle."

"Oh, right, by that you mean some spoiled, arrogant, ditzy-deb that carries a fluffy little dog around everywhere she goes?"

"Precisely!"

"As wonderful as that sounds Sebastian I'll put my money on Evie. In fact I'm taking her to the house in the Hamptons this weekend to meet mom and dad so they can see how wonderful she is in person"

"First of all; you don't have any money; your family does. And secondly; Please let me come; I'm dying to see this little disaster play out."

"What are you, a ten year old schoolgirl or something? When did you become such a gossip monger?"

"Michael I'm hurt and insulted; if you were paying attention you'd know that I've always been a gossip monger....and the schoolgirl outfit thing only happened twice and I was hopelessly drunk both times"

"You worry me sometimes Sebastian; but nonetheless ok yes you can come but do not bring Eleanor"

"And why not!"

"Oh I don't know, I'm thinking perhaps it's possibly the fact that my mom would go berserk if you showed up with anyone other than your wife Sessile, that's why!"

"So what? I'm a grown man and can cavort with anyone I choose!"

"And then my mom calls your mom to tell her all about it!"

"So what time shall Sessile and I show up?"

"Saturday at noon"

"Done"

During the drive home all Mike could think about was his discussion with Sebastian; he knew full well that his old friend was right; his parents would never accept Evie and in all likelihood were just tolerating the situation until Mike came to his senses and was ready to settle down with Abigail Fontaine; the dull witted doggy carrying daughter of a Manhattan socialite and close friend of Mike's mom.

Mike and Abby had been out on a date the previous year but it was purely a product of his mom meddling and playing matchmaker and Mike agreeing to one date so she would stop cornering him in the kitchen every time he went over there and doing her sales presentation which should have been entitled The Wonders of Abby.

He got the impression that his and Abby's parents would be the only real beneficiaries of the 'merger' if he suddenly lost his mind and agreed to date and marry her...and her dog.

The date in his estimation was a complete and utter waste of time; Abby made it clear that physical romance was very much a possibility that night and was essentially counting on it as a tool to snare her prey but Mike would have none of it.

For some reason she reminded him of Paris Hilton which was essentially the equivalent of putting salt peter on his steak tartar and never being able to have a respectable erection again.

Mike didn't want Abby or anyone else; he wanted Evie; and if his parents weren't willing to accept her he knew he would have a seemingly insurmountable problem on his hands.

Chapter 8

Mike pulled up to the curb in front of Evie's building in his freshly washed sparkling silver Mercedes SLK at 7am sharp on Saturday morning to collect her for their weekend in the country.

As he sat there in his car talking on his cell phone to a friend Evie emerged through the front doors of the building and stood up on the stoop signaling him to come help with her bags but he didn't see her.

She gave up and dragged one of the suitcases packed full of clothes and shoes down the steps to his car. He still hadn't noticed her so she tapped on the passenger side window to get his attention at which time he jumped out to lend a hand.

"I've been signaling you from the stoop for five minutes to come help me mister!"

Of course it had only been a few seconds and there was little chance of him seeing her from that particular angle but for some reason she was determined to make him feel a little guilty 'just because' as women sometimes like to do for no apparent reason, at least none that a man would be interested in discussing or trying to understand.

But Mike, as usual, was on his game and didn't miss a beat;

"My apologies! The extra set of eyes I have in the side of my head aren't working today...the repairman should be coming by later; they make house calls in the Hamptons"

"Ha, ha... drole Michael; now will you help me with my bags please?"

She was quite surprised at herself; she had never used the word *drole* before and was almost starting to sound like Mike and his rich friends; she liked the feeling of fitting in and being one of them; or at least thinking she was.

"Wow, are you sure you have enough suitcases? Maybe we should go back upstairs and pack a few more; wouldn't want to forget anything; actually, you know Jane; I could just order a truck and driver to transport it all for you...maybe someone to pack and unpack for you as well?"

A few minutes later Evie thought to herself "no need, I already have someone" as she lit a cigarette and smiled as Mike struggled up and down the steps with the luggage.

Mike tried to act like a porter and tipped his hat smiling as he passed her while going up and down the steps; Evie was quite amused by it but perhaps not for the same reason that he had intended.

As she stood there chuckling at Mike's buffoonery a loud but mildly familiar *"Hey!"* resonated from just behind Eve.

She turned to see who the big voice belonged to.

"Tom, what are you doing here?"

"I'm stalking you" he said with a straight face.

Eve looked horrified for a moment but then realized that he's not the type even though she joked about it that evening in the smoking room with Lena…then it occurred to her that Samantha must have told him every horrible word she had said about him.

He chuckled and immediately continued *"I walk by here every day on my way to work"*

"But it's Saturday" Eve said as if she was actually under the impression that work only happens during business hours on Monday to Friday. She of course was quite aware that people in city maintenance and retail and so forth work on weekends but was simply making a point about their respective stations in life; the trouble was she really didn't intend to do that; it just slipped out.

"What's the difference? When ya gotta work ya gotta work….who gives a shit what day it is?"

"You're right; Tom, look, I've been meaning to talk to you about a few things; I'm sorry about that thing at the restaurant between your girlfriend and I; it was terribly rude of me and I'm sorry"

"No big deal; it really doesn't matter one way or another does it?"

"Well it matters to me! I said some really mean things about you in the smoking room with Samantha standing right there and I feel just horrible about it"

"Horrible for the fact that Sam heard it all or sorry for saying it at all; you'll have to forgive me, I'm from a small town so I'm a little slow"

She wanted to say more as she sensed Tom's obvious sarcasm and hostility but her efforts were cut short as Mike came around after loading the last bag into the car; *"Who's your friend Eve?"* extending his hand to Tom; *"Mike Dubrow, pleased to meet you!"*

"Tom O'Neil...how ya doin' bud"

Tom grasped Mike's soft manicured hand with his much larger powerful calloused hand. As soon as their hands made contact it was on; dominance had to be established. Sensing that Mike was trying to squeeze his hand a little too hard Tom effortlessly put the squeeze on so hard that a crack could be heard twenty feet away.

Mike winced and all three of them looked at each other but said nothing.

Mike did his best to try and conceal the fact that his hand was injured and simply reverted to instinct and did what he did best; kept talking;

"Didn't we meet at Lance Fontaine's party a few months ago? You're a broker aren't you?"

"No, I'm a sewer worker"

Mike broke out in laughter; *"sewer worker, that's a good one; no really, how's the stock biz these days; any inside tips I should know about?"*

"You're not listening bud, I'm a sewer worker; something wrong with that?"

"If I've offended you I apologize...."

"Have a nice day...see ya around Eve"

Tom turned and walked away.

Evie caught herself lingering for a moment watching him as if she had just met him for the first time.

Mike and Evie hopped in the car and drove off. Once outside the city Mike started to inquire about the mysterious newcomer to their little love game.

"I must say, your friend's a little cranky this morning don't you think?"

"He's got his reasons"

"Like?"

"Like I said some really nasty things about him to a friend of his and it really hurt his feelings"

"So where do you know him from?"

"We went out once and he's a family friend of Sue's"

"Handsome fellow...rugged looking"

"I hadn't noticed and can we change the subject now please?"

"I'd like nothing better my dear; consider it changed! So how about a little travelling music, anything in particular? Everything sounds great in here; I had the sound system beefed up when I leased the car"

Mike started rambling off numbers and technical statistics regarding the sound system plus a bunch of words that ended in 'hertz' but Eve interrupted with a simple yet decisive; *"Got any country?"*

Mike almost gasped in horror at the prospect of country music playing on the premium sound system in his Mercedes but found Evie a country station on the radio without delay or commentary regarding her musical taste; he fully intended to enjoy it no matter how much he detested it and immediately made a mental note to buy some country music CD's to have on hand in the car for subsequent trips with Eve.

By the time they reached the Long Island area all thoughts of Tom were gone and the two continued on as if nothing had happened. But they both knew that something did; they just weren't quite sure what it was yet.

They finally arrived at the family retreat in prestigious Westhampton just before noon to find a bevy of expensive cars in the massive parking area in front of the estate scattered around a central fountain by the garages.

"Are you sure the house is big enough Mick? I don't know, maybe you should build an addition or something...I really expected something much larger and am a little disappointed"

Evie of course was just kidding; the house was the largest home she had ever seen let alone actually been to. It was a bona fide Westhampton mansion; approximately 30,000 square feet of living space and had been in Mike's family for over eighty years.

The house sat on a hundred acres and had horse stables, indoor and outdoor swimming pools, state of the art exercise facility, massive theatre room, bowling alley, twenty bedrooms and a small staff of twelve to look after it all.

Mike played along and said; *"Yeah, I was thinking the same thing; I'll mention your idea to father over dinner...it does get a little crowded around here on weekends"*

"Geez Mick I was just kidding"

"No no, I think we should discuss it with father and actually get everyone's input over dinner"

"Don't you dare!"

"What's this? The gutsy miss Evie has lost her nerve?.... Impossible!....I'm just playing with you...relax my dear"

"Imagine what your family would think of me if you actually told them that I said that. They would think I was an absolutely horrible person"

"Actually you might just fit right in; most of the girls in our social circle are spoiled and demanding and wouldn't hesitate to say something like that believe it or not; they are very adept at whining and complaining. In many cases it's all they're good at"

"But I'm not from your social circle and even if I was I wouldn't say something like that; and for the record this really is the biggest house I've ever seen in my life; to be honest I actually thought it was a school or a hotel or something when we pulled in; it's absolutely magnificent!"

"Well thank you; so why don't we go inside so I can give you the grand tour"

"I'm scared! What if they hate me because I'm just a commoner?"

"Then I guess that would be their loss: you just be your adorable witty self and don't worry about them"

They hopped out of the car and Evie went around to the trunk to collect her bags.

"What are you doing Eve?"

"Well I'd like to get my bags but in order for that to happen you're going to have to open the trunk lid Ludwig"

"No no, no, my dear; we don't carry our own bags here; someone will take them up to your room for you"

"My room? What happened to 'our' room?"

"It wouldn't be appropriate for us to stay in the same room unless we were married"

"Oh?"

"But don't worry, my room is right next to yours... with an adjoining door" he said while wriggling his eyebrows and winking suggestively.

Eve was a little surprised that they wouldn't share the same room as after all they were both adults.

Mike could tell by her facial expression that she was a little put off and interjected;

"Eve, it's just protocol; a matter of appearances and etiquette; no one cares if one of us stays in the others room all night peeling down the wallpaper and screaming like banshee's as long as we don't discuss it; we don't discuss things around here by the way; we simply repress and endure"

"I see"

"Now you really didn't think I'd be able to stay away from you all night did you?"

"You better not mister and you better not leave me alone in there with them either!"

"I know you're uncomfortable with this whole thing and I don't want you to be; they're just people; strip away the money and all the 'stuff' and they're really no different than anyone else"

Of course Eve knew nothing could be further from the truth but didn't attempt to debate it as it simply wasn't the right time for that particular discussion; but she did appreciate Mike's effort to make her feel more at home.

Evie braced herself for the big plunge and took a deep breath as Mike pushed open the front door to find the family butler Waddington standing there waiting for them;

"Greetings Master Michael, I trust you had a pleasant trip"

"We did indeed Waddington, thank you; please have someone take Miss Evie's bags up to her room"

"Right away sir; shall I have the kitchen prepare a meal for you?"

"We're fine; that will be all Waddington"

"Very good sir; so pleased to meet you Miss Evie;"

"Likewise, thank you"

Eve wasn't really sure what to say to him or what to call him; she had never seen a real butler before.

Paul Kool

"There's my baby!" A voice sang from the opposite end of the grand entry hall.

It was Mike's mom; she strode over to him and gave him a big hug still wearing her equestrian riding gear.

"And this lovely young lady must be Evie yes?"

"Yes maam" Evie said not quite sure to curtsey or shake hands or just stand there trembling inside with fear.

"Oh let's not be so formal; you just call me Betsy...or Bets if you like"

"Yes maam, I mean Betsy"

"Please excuse my attire my dear, a few of us were out for a refreshing morning horse ride and I haven't had a moment to change; do you ride?"

"Yes I do, I grew up in a small town and our neighbor had a horse farm so I had the opportunity to ride often"

"How quaint! See? We already have something in common; we'll have to take a ride together tomorrow to get better acquainted but first things first; I'll take you up to your room so you can get settled; that's a lovely sweater Eve"

"Thank you Betsy"

"Michael, your father is with Sebastian in the study"

Betsy took Evie by the hand and they disappeared up the giant winding staircase leading to the bedrooms on the second floor chatting like two long lost friends.

It was the complete opposite of how Eve thought things would play out; she anticipated catty comments and a cool reception at best.

As Mike was about to enter the study the door flung open and he found himself face to face with Sebastian.

"So there you are; I was wondering when you were going to show up old boy"

"Sebastian, it's precisely ten minutes after twelve; that hardly qualifies as tardiness; when did you and Sessile arrive?"

"We got here early"

"In anticipation of the impending 'disaster' as you put it I gather?"

"Absolutely!"

"Well I hate to disappoint you my dear old annoying friend but mom just met Evie and they are upstairs together right now getting Eve settled in; and chatting like old friends"

"Of course they are; your mom is just being cordial; it doesn't mean you have her blessing to marry Evie or anything of the sort"

"We'll see about that"

"Michael is that you?"

It was Mike's dad calling him from inside the study.

"Are you going to stand out there all day or come in?"

"Coming" he said rolling his eyes to alleviate the tension that always emerged whenever they spoke.

On his way in he said to Sebastian; *"how about a ride on the trail bikes later?"*

"Absolutely!"

Mike went in to find his father sitting behind his big mahogany desk smoking a cigar;

"Would you like one son?"

"Actually yes, I'd love one thank you"

"So how are things?" he said as he poured them both a glass of scotch neat.

Mike settled into a big leather chair in front of the desk and reached out to receive his drink;

"Thanks; ummm, work is going well; landed some big accounts; say, this isn't going to lead into the 'come and work for me' discussion again is it?"

"No, we'll save that for the day common sense prevails and you're all grown up!"

"I thought we weren't going to have this discussion"

Mike's dad laughed; *"I had no intention of doing so; you're the one that mentioned it...I'm simply responding to your comment"*

"You're right dad, I apologize; I'm just a little tense"

"Why so?"

"Not sure what the reaction would be to Evie"

"Well that depends on what your intentions are I suppose; Sebastian tells me you're quite smitten with this young lady"

"For once Sebastian is right; she's incredible; there's no other word for it...you'll see for yourself shortly; she's upstairs with mom unpacking her things"

"Sebastian also tells me she's not from our social circle and has more than a few skeletons in her closet; you do realize of course that these types of things might be problematic for the family; could cast us in a bad light; hurt business relations; and of course you realize you have certain obligations regarding your choice of spouse so getting too serious may not be in your best interest...but you go ahead and have your fun for now; I was young once myself you know so I understand"

"Well, thank you for that, father; that's very reassuring; but she's not a play toy; with all due respect I care very deeply for her; it doesn't matter where she comes from; she is a wonderful person and I thank god every single day for the privilege of knowing her and having her in my life"

"Michael you'll meet a lot of girls that want to be in your life; but you have to consider the fact that they may be more interested in our money and lifestyle than anything else"

"Yes, of course father, why didn't I see that; of course they wouldn't be interested in me for any other reason; it's just the money; well thank you for the clarification

and the assessment of my value in life as a human being; very refreshing indeed; I'm going to find Evie"

"Watch your tone son; you best be careful; I won't have this family or our reputation put at risk"

"Or what?...what are you going to do cut me off and throw me out of the city apartment?...go right ahead; but do me one favor father; at least make an effort to see Evie for who she is before you make assumptions about her"

"You're not understanding me son; it doesn't matter if she's the most wonderful person in the world; it only matters where she comes from"

"And where did great great grandma come from?"

"What do you mean by that?"

"You think I don't know that she was one of the server girls at the club?"

"We're not having this discussion today!"

"So when will it be a good time father; shall I make an appointment with your secretary?"

"That's enough Michael!"

"Yes, you're right as always father; it is enough! Enough of your highbrow upper crust bullshit"

Mike left his father's study promptly after their exchange of pleasantries and took the service elevator to the second level to join Evie.

"Hey, Jane....it's me....open up..." Mike said as he knocked eagerly on Evie's bedroom door.

"Who is it?"

"It's me, Mike"

"I'm sorry I don't know anyone by that name"

"How about Mick?"

"Yes I do vaguely remember meeting someone by that name; the door is unlocked silly, just come in"

Mike went in and stopped dead in his tracks. Evie was lying on the bed in nothing but a cammy and a pair of tiny black lace panties.

This was another one of those rare instances where Mike had nothing to say; he stood there for a moment gazing at her as if trying to decide whether she was real or some carnal apparition; then rushed over in a frenzy like a kid in a candy store;

"Oh Evie, you are so incredibly beautiful"

She gently pulled him closer and they began to kiss.

"Wait Mick...the door...did you lock it?"

"Shit"

He clumsily stumbled back to the door and locked it while simultaneously trying to unbutton his shirt with one hand and pull his arm out of the sleeve; done; next sleeve; shirt off; now the pants.

He had almost made it back to the bed and had already almost managed to get one leg out of his pants when there was a knock on the door; it was Sessile.

"Evie dahling; it's Sessile; I just wanted to say hello and see if you need anything"

Mike hopped around on one foot trying desperately to get out of his jeans but lost his footing and fell into the night table by the bed knocking over the lamp in a frenzy of excitement;

"Is everything alright in there Evie?"

Mike spoke up from his position on the floor, still working on getting his right foot out of the pant leg;

"Not a good time Sessile!"

"I was hoping to come in and chat with Evie for a few moments and get acquainted"

"Not now Sessile!" Mike said again as he sat on his butt on the floor next to the bed trying desperately to get his foot out of his pant leg with the shoe still on. Then to make matters worse another familiar voice manifested from out in the hallway to further annoy him;

"Mike...it's Sebastian; I was wondering if you were ready to take the trail bikes out for a ride yet?"

"I'm not ready for the trail bikes but I am getting ready to murder the both of you if you don't go away this second!"

"Why? What are you two up to in there? I hope there's nothing lascivious going on; mother wouldn't approve; perhaps I should have her come up...Eve, is Michael trying to take advantage of you in there?"

As Mike made his way to the door now in his underwear ready to blast the two for the interruption he could hear Sebastian and Sessile snickering and trying to contain their laughter; at that point his suspicions were confirmed; his old friends were simply having a few laughs at their expense; perhaps an initiation of sorts for Eve.

But of course by then the magic of the moment had passed; the passion would have to wait until later so they simply opted to clean up, change, and go downstairs to join the others.

When they arrived they found Mikes parents, his older brothers and their wives and children, his grandmother, his sister and her family, his uncle and a few family friends all sitting in the grand family room enjoying drinks by a fireplace big enough to park a small car in.

Evie felt like dying; it was tantamount to facing a firing squad.

"Well well well; Michael said you were lovely but that appears to have been the understatement of the century; Mike Dubrow senior; very pleased to finally meet you" Mikes father said as he extended his hand to Evie.

"Thank you sir, it's a pleasure to meet you as well"

Mikes mom proceeded to pull Evie around the room by the hand and introduce her to everyone. Although they were all very gracious Evie felt more out of place than ever before. But true to form she maintained her composure throughout…she also knew a thing or two about having to repress and endure.

After a few minutes Mike decided it was time to rescue his damsel in distress;

"I think it's time I borrow my lovely Evie if you all don't mind and give her the grand tour of our humble home"

"Dinner is at five in the dining room; don't be late you two"

"Ok mother, we'll be back in time"

As they left the room they could hear them all talking; "she's delightful" "very striking young lady" and a bevy of other flattering comments. Things were suddenly going much better than Eve had anticipated.

Mike and Eve ran into Sessile and Sebastian on their way out;

"Well I hope you two had your fun" Mike said still a little annoyed with the pair for ruining his romantic tryst earlier.

"Sorry old boy, couldn't resist; all in good fun…you understand"

"Yes, I understand fully…and Sebastian?"

"yes Michael"

"remind me to kill you later will you?"

"Absolutely!" Sebastian laughed.

"Hello Eve I'm Sebastian's wife Sessile; sorry about all of that upstairs earlier; we were just having a little fun; I hope you're not offended."

"Not at all; it was actually quite funny watching Mick here hopping around with one leg out of his pants and crashing into the night table"

"Is that what that noise was?"

"Yes unfortunately"

Sessile and Evie chuckled.

Mike cut in; *"Well as much as I'm enjoying this little trip down memory lane I'm going to steal Evie away now and show her around the grounds...with no further interruption from the likes of you two troublemakers; are we clear?"*

"Absolutely!"

After Mike and Evie left the house Sessile and Sebastian had a little chat of their own;

"What in God's name are you doing Sessile?"

"What do you mean by that?"

"I thought we had an agreement; you were to give Evie a hard time and help get rid of her"

"But they have pet names"

"So what the hell does that mean?"

"You're such a boy; don't you understand anything? Pet names means it's really serious"

"I know it's serious; that's the problem...and I have a pet name for you as well"

"That's so sweet, what is it?"

"Traitor!"

"Oh how amusing indeed Sebastian; your multifarious wit continues to bore the shit out of me; look, call me what you will but I like her; she's not at all how you described her; I think she's adorable; and very witty... and her taste in clothes is impeccable...did you see that beautiful top she had on?"

"oh yes, it's all I could think about; in fact if I don't find out where she bought it I'm not going to sleep for a week"

"Stop making jokes Sebastian; this is serious"

"Of course it's serious; I don't want Michael to get hurt; nothing good can come from this unholy union of class and commoner; it's not a good mix Sessile and you know it; now you better start helping me sabotage this thing for Michaels sake"

"I will do nothing of the sort! I think she's just what Michael needs; did you see the way they looked at each other? I don't want any part of this little scheme of yours

and if you don't cut it out I'm going to tell Michael all about it and he's going to be very angry with you; and I'll tell your mother as well; so stay out of it Sebastian; I mean it!"

Sebastian just walked off grumbling and joined the others in the family room for drinks.

After a lovely walk around the grounds and a chat by the stream Eve and Mike returned to the house to prepare for dinner. As they washed up in Eve's en-suite bathroom she gasped in horror;

"Oh my god Michael; look at your hand; it's so swollen... what happened?"

"I think your friend Tom squeezed a little too hard; I was hoping it would feel better by now but it seems to be getting worse unfortunately"

"That son of a bitch! I'm going to give him a piece of my mind when we get home; and you should have said something earlier!"

"I didn't want to spoil your weekend; it was going so well"

"You have to see a doctor; we're leaving"

"We can't just leave like this...what will the others think?"

"I don't give a damn what they think; we're leaving! When your mom see's your hand she will fully understand; and be pretty upset I might add; we need to get you to a doctor immediately; sit here and I'll pack my things"

A few moments later they went downstairs into the kitchen and Eve made up an icepack for Mikes hand and left him waiting there while she went to get his mom.

Eve causally walked over to Mike's mom who was in the great room conversing with some of the guests;

"Betsy, I'm sorry to interrupt but could we please speak in the kitchen for a moment?"

"Of course dear" she excused herself and the two strode off to the kitchen.

"Oh my! Michael; what happened to your hand?"

Despite the icepack the swelling persisted and his hand was now turning purple and blue; in all likelihood it was broken in at least a couple of places.

He didn't give his mom a direct answer regarding the cause as he didn't want to admit that he was 'out-squeezed' in a handshake domination duel by a common sewer worker.

"Gosh, I'd call Dr. Kline but he's in Nassau for a month so I'm afraid there's little we can do here; unless one of the guests knows another doctor that can come"

"Not to worry Betsy, I'll drive Mike back to the city and take him to the emergency department at Mount Sinai hospital; I'll take good care of him"

"I'm quite confident that you will Evie; Thank you so much dear; you two call me tomorrow; promise?"

"Yes maam...I mean Betsy"

Waddington saw to it that Eve's bags were put in the car and the two left for the city shortly thereafter.

"So what do you think?" Mike said as they drove along on their journey back to the city.

"About?"

"The recent turbulence on the Tokyo stock market; the visit of course you silly girl"

"Well Mick, I hate to say it but you were right again; they did actually seem to be like regular people; quite nice actually...especially your mom and grandma...they made me feel right at home"

"Yeah, they really took to you; you are actually the first girl I've ever brought to the country house so I'm sure they realize that there is something special going on between us"

"Well I'm glad we made the trip; it was nice, thank you for taking me"

"My pleasure; I'm just sorry we had to cut it short because of my hand"

"Well I have a few choice words for Tom...that was a horrible thing to do"

"Actually it's not his fault Eve; I tried to squeeze his hand quite hard; it's a guy thing; dominance and all that; but I didn't realize how powerful he was and...well... this is the end result; I shouldn't engage in that kind of activity with blue collar workers; they're obviously used to physical exertion so unfortunately I'm no match for

them in the physical strength department...please don't blame him"

"Well I do. He could plainly see that you aren't one of the rough and tumble guys that he works with and should have been more considerate; typical of people from his social class"

Chapter 9

"Get your ass out here mister!" Evie shouted as she pounded on the front door of Tom's house in Queens a few nights after the acute episode of *weekendus interruptus* at Mike's family estate.

She pounded and pounded but no answer; only his dog barking.

"Come on out here you chicken shit sonovabitch Thomas O'Neil!"

Tom suddenly materialized from behind her;

"Chicken shit? Wow, I haven't heard that one since grade six; you should stay more current with your insults; that one's a little dated"

"Grade six huh? When do you graduate?"

"See? With just a little effort you're getting better already...'when do you graduate'...that was pretty

good...but...hey, enough reminiscing; what the hell do you want!"

"Where did you come from?"

"A small town in the Midwest....how about yourself?"

"That's not what I meant...but yeah....me too"

"Super! Look I've had a long day waist deep in shit water fancy pants; I'm going inside. You can either come in or you can stand out here alone and entertain the neighbors; but they've got guns so if they don't like your act things could get messy; ya might want to take off those pretty little high heel shoes of yours in case you have to run"

Evie was apprehensive about going inside but Tom acted like he didn't care; he simply unlocked his door and walked into the house leaving the screen door open behind him.

She started talking to him through the screen door.

He switched on the TV and turned up the volume to drown her out with a big smile on his face; *"Ah, better already!"*

This of course wasn't typical behavior for Tom; he was normally considerate and courteous but after hearing about the horrible things she said about him to Samantha and having to hear about other derogatory comments she had made to a few mutual acquaintances his patients had quite simply run out where she was concerned and decided that if she was going to act like a spoiled child then he'd simply treat her accordingly.

"Stop avoiding me Tom"

"Well then stop heating the damn neighborhood! Unlike you and your rich boyfriend I don't have money to throw away; that front door is going to close in about ten seconds; you had better choose which side of it you want to be on right quick; you're in or you're out... what's it gonna be princess?"

Evie went inside.

"Don't mind the dog; he won't hurt you" Tom said as his dog jumped up on Eve to greet her.

"I love dogs! What's his name?" Evie said while chuckling and playing with him.

"Eddy; and he seems to like you; he doesn't know any better"

Eve stood up obviously ignoring that particular comment and said;

"Why did you have to do that to Mike?"

"Do what?"

"You broke his hand"

"I'm makin spaghetti for dinner; stayin?"

"Answer me!"

"I'd love to engage in witty banter about your little boyfriend...what was his name again, Nancy or something like that? I have to take a shower; watch the boiling water on the stove for me will ya?"

"I will not!"

"Whatever!"

He removed his enormous construction boots and placed them on the mat by the front door and started pulling off his shirt as he headed off into the bedroom.

A moment later Eve could hear the shower turn on and Tom singing; quite badly I might add but obviously enjoying himself regardless...particularly since he was doing it on purpose to annoy her.

It didn't work; Evie was too upset and nervous to be annoyed by the singing as she sat on a chair at the kitchen table drumming her fingers on the table while humming along to Tom's bad singing over the noise of the TV set as if afraid to move around the room or touch anything in fear of contracting an incurable case of the cooties.

But as she scanned the living and dining room from her perch she was quite surprised to see that the house was neat and actually clean as well; cootie free in fact!

She had imagined a smelly unkempt hovel with dirty dishes stacked to the ceiling and bugs crawling around the filth as the "Hoarders" film crew waited eagerly in anticipation outside the front door for the signal to burst in and cure terrible Tom of his apparent psychological disorder.

But the reality of the situation was that she found Tom's home charming clean and comfortable; much to her disappointment.

The water started to boil over; she wanted to just leave it alone to spite Tom but turned it down instead and carefully approached the bathroom door.

"Where do you keep the pasta?" she shouted from behind the door afraid to touch it. No answer.

She tried again *"Tom; where is the pasta?"*

Suddenly without warning the bathroom door flung open and Tom was standing there in nothing but a towel around his waist; Eve found it very hard to hate him at that particular moment…she was too busy gawking at his chiseled physique.

Evie stepped back obviously startled but yet couldn't take her eyes off him for a long and apparently quite enjoyable few seconds.

"Looking for something?" Tom said in a causal tone of voice knowing full well she was getting an eyeful.

"Looking for? I'm not looking at…I mean for anything mister!"

"Didn't I hear you say something about pasta a minute ago?….for the spaghetti?….is that what you were hollering about? Top cupboard above the stove"

"Yes, of course!....I'm just going to put it in to cook"

"...and she can even boil water ladies and gentlemen... what a catch!" Tom quipped sarcastically as he disappeared into the bedroom.

He reemerged moments later dressed in blue jeans and a white t-shirt; clean shaven and smelling of Brute aftershave lotion.

"You still here?...gee this must be serious" he said chuckling while opening the fridge to get a beer and throwing one to Eve without any warning other than the word "catch" as the can hurtled towards her like a missile.

Much to his surprise she actually caught it with ease.

"Sorry Eve, I know it's not the fine wine or champagne someone of your social standing and superior breeding is used to but it's all I got"

"I'll have you know I've had beer many times before and I like it just fine"

"I'm glad; I would have lost sleep over it tonight otherwise" Tom said as he opened a can of spaghetti sauce with one of those manual hand operated openers.

"Drole!...that means..."

"I know what it means fancy pants...it means you like to use words that make you sound like something you're not!"

"Clever; I still want to know why you did that to Mike"

"He started it; I finished it; simple"

"What do you mean he started it; he just extended his hand in friendship to you"

"What a fucking load of horseshit! He was trying to put the squeeze on me to show me what a big man he is in front of you and how much better than me he is with his fancy clothes and Mercedes so I just gave him a taste of his own medicine and squeezed back; how was I supposed to know he was such a little girl"

"Oh, so you're punishing him because he has a good job and money?"

"Yeah, that's about the size of it; uh huh...that and the fact that he's an arrogant spoiled little dick...you two are made for each other...good luck with that!"

"Wow, that's really mature!"

"You know something fancy pants; you're absolutely right; it was incredibly immature of me; I should have waited until he went to a local club to ambush him and pour beer all over him in front of everyone and then talk shit about him behind his back to everyone even though I don't know the first fucking thing about the guy...you're right; that would have definitely been the mature thing to do!"

She had no response to that one.

They both just stood there in his kitchen staring each other down for a full couple of minutes like a couple of cowboys at the OK Corral; then they both broke out in laughter realizing how silly they had both been.

"Oh boy...what a pair we are....where's your plates?"

"I don't have any; Eddy and I can't afford them so we just eat off the floor; geez I don't know I'm guessing there's plates in the cupboard where people usually keep them; but ok....look; truce; I guess we both overreacted a little; so at least stay and eat and then we can fight some more or you can leave or whatever"

"I may as well stay; the evening is a write-off now anyway"

"Well I'm glad I'm here to amuse you and fill your time"

"I didn't mean it like that and you know it!"

"How the hell would I know what you mean or don't mean? And speaking of wasted time; where's Lady Mercedes tonight...no candlelit dinner at 'chez snob in the exclusive asshole section?"

"That was last night thank you very much! And for your information he's at home taking care of his hand...and you could make an effort to be a little nicer to him"

"Why in the name of Christ would I want to do that? Are we playing racquetball together this weekend or will I be bumping into him at the social club?....in case you haven't noticed we travel in different circles...and I'm

guessing he won't be doing much with that hand for a while anyway; I betcha he's sitting in that fancy condo of his right now being waited on hand and foot like the little Nancy boy he is"

"How do you know where he lives?"

"I'm a stalker remember? Isn't that what you called me? I've been following him around day and night hiding in the shadows waiting to pounce like Jack the Ripper; the hand was just a preview of what I've got in store for him; come on Eve! Think, all those executive types live in expensive condos in Manhattan don't they? Even a lowly mentally deficient common worker like me can figure that one out"

"Sorry"

"Listen fancy pants, I'll tell ya something; if had someone that looked like you for a girlfriend I wouldn't let a broken hand stop me from seeing you; fuck I broke my entire left arm two years ago after losing my footing in a service tunnel; had it reset and finished my shift...I didn't sit around like baby crying over it"

"Well aren't you tough...and do you really need to cuss in every second sentence?"

"You just bring out the best in me I guess"

"Well if that's the best I'd hate to see the worst"

"Stick around, maybe you'll get lucky"

"You are such an ass!"

"Yeah, and you're a stuck up little hillbilly that thinks she's all that with her fancy clothes and big city job!"

"Yeah, you think so huh?"

"Yeah, that's what I think and I'll tell ya something else; what you need little lady is a good spanking to remind you of where you come from and to teach you some manners"

"Don't you dare touch me!"

"Don't flatter yourself!"

"You disgust me!"

"And you disgust me even more!"

Without warning Eve leapt into Tom's arms and they made love like two sex starved animals in heat; on the kitchen table; on the sofa; in the bathroom and in the bedroom. It went on for almost two full hours until they were totally and utterly...satisfied.

Then they heated up their cold spaghetti in the microwave and sat down to eat as if nothing happened.

"Say something will you?"

"I'm sorry, how inconsiderate of me; ummm...thank you for the wonderful sex Eve; I especially liked the part on the kitchen countertop"

"That's not what I meant but it's better than silence; I don't know what just happened but I don't do things like that....I don't even know you"

"Well I guess ya do now so you're going to just have to suck it up princess. But it doesn't matter anyway because whatever I do I'll never meet your high standards and expectations so let's just write it off as a mistake and forget about it"

"Yes, let's do that; you won't tell Mike will you?"

"Yeah, I'm going to rush right over to his place like a little gossip queen and tell him all about it while we braid each other's hair after the pillow fight; No Eve, don't worry; I'm not so desperate for your love that I'd stoop that low...I mean yeah, I've got to admit that the sex was pretty damn amazing but let's face it, your personality needs a lot of work....way too high maintenance for me...frankly my dear you're a pain in the ass!"

"What the hell does that mean?"

"I thought it was pretty self-explanatory"

"I'll have you know there are plenty of guys that are just dying to date me"

"Yeah I've seen the type of guys you date; they're not guys, they're department store mannequins with sweaters draped over their shoulders tied off at the front holding tennis racquets with names like Biff and Randall" he said while doing a series of department store mannequin poses.

Evie couldn't help it; she had to laugh; it was actually quite funny.

"Careful, you don't want to have to admit that terrible Tom made you laugh or that there's a human being under all that armor"

"Don't get used to it big boy....anyway, I have to go; so thank you so much for dinner and the....recreational activities"

"Oh you mean the sex?....it's ok to say it you know; actually why don't we go outside in the yard and announce it with a bullhorn so the entire neighborhood can hear; I'm sure none of them have ever had sex before"

"Don't you dare!"

"Don't worry; I wouldn't want you to leave here feeling any less repressed and uptight than you did when you arrived"

He got her again; she chuckled; perhaps as much at the comments as being pleasantly surprised by his sense of humor and keen wit.

"Listen Tom I really am sorry that I said all those things about you in front of Samantha and pouring beer on her wasn't the best course of action in retrospect"

"Yeah.....but you gotta admit it felt good!"

"Well that's a horrible thing to say about your girlfriend and speaking of which why isn't she here filling your living room with the suffocating scent of her perfume; Street Whore by Chanel"

"Good one fancy pants; but I'm not seeing her anymore and I gotta admit; the beer thing was kind of funny...so what did she do to piss you off so badly?"

"I don't know....anyway, I'm sorry and I really should be getting home but I hope we can be friends regardless of what has happened"

"You know where to find me if you wanna talk or ... anything else!" Tom said wriggling his eyebrows and again scoring points by making eve blush and giggle.

Eve got her coat, stepped into her high heels and headed for the front door.

"What, no goodnight kiss?" Tom shouted in jest from the couch as he tried to find the hockey game on TV.

"That would entail you getting up off the couch and walking over here"

"Drole!"

Evie played with the dog for a couple of minutes and left: she drove straight home while muttering things like "oh my god...what the hell am I doing" and the ever popular "fuck, I must be out of my goddamn mind!"

Chapter 10

The minute Eve hopped in her car after leaving Tom's house she called Susan and Lena to set up a lunch date for the next day.

She didn't tell them what had happened but they could sense something was amiss right away; but the 'something' they had imagined was more along the lines of a marriage proposal from Mike or news of his much anticipated infidelity; not a hot romp in the hay with terrible Tom the sewer guy.

Eve did not sleep well at all that night; it's doubtful that anyone in her position would. She was experiencing a good deal of guilt over what had taken place and felt as if she had betrayed Mike and possibly undermined a chance at real happiness for the first time in her life.

But on the other hand she also considered the fact that they had just started seeing each other and no official consensus had been reached or indicated as of yet with regard to exclusivity; all they had essentially agreed to do was continue to see each other romantically and see where it goes. This didn't make her feel any better.

Despite her sassy brash demeanor Eve wasn't the type of girl to just hop into bed with any guy she hardly knew...this was completely out of character as she wasn't looking for meaningless sex; she was looking for love.

And this was essentially the crux of the problem she was having reconciling her actions and feelings where Tom was concerned. Why on earth would she have sexual relations with a guy she doesn't even like and hardly know?

The obvious answer was that she did in fact have strong emotional and romantic feelings for Tom but she wasn't prepared to acknowledge it or simply wasn't consciously aware of it.

She paced back and forth in her tiny yet ultra-stylish loft apartment from her bedroom area to her living room, which was all of about twenty five feet, drinking coffee after coffee while mumbling to herself;

"Nice going Eve! Crappers! How could I make such a mess of this? Mike has been so wonderful and kind and his mom and grandma were so nice to me; they allowed me into their home and I repaid them for their kindness by sleeping with a sewer worker behind their backs like a common streetwalker; I'm a horrible dirty girl; that's all there is to it; I'm so ashamed; damn you Tom! Why did you have to screw everything up! I should have

never gone to see him and left well enough alone; but no; I had to stick my nose in"

She finally fell asleep on her sofa at about 4am when the caffeine went AWOL and woke to the sound of her radio alarm at 6am and a formidable coffee stain on her area rug; she apparently fell asleep with the mug still in hand and the coffee apparently seized the opportunity to escape;

"Great! This is the second mess I've managed to create in the last 24 hours" she declared as she looked in the mirror applying her makeup; *"nice going!"*

She had absolutely no idea how she would possibly be able to face Mike after what she had done. She briefly even considered just throwing caution to the wind and telling him the truth and dealing with the consequences; and at least feel a little better for being honest about it. After agonizing over it all the way to the office she finally decided against it.

"Wow, you look like shit" Gail quipped as she brought Eve her morning coffee and messages.

"Well thank you Gail"

"Are you ok? You look like you haven't slept in days"

"I'm perfectly fine Gail; that will be all"

"Why do I even bother to ask?" Gail said jokingly as she strode out of Eve's office.

Eve started going through her messages nervously anticipating the inevitability of having to look Mike in the eye within the hour or possibly even sooner.

Sooner came first!

"Good morning sunshine!" Mike said as he bounced into Eve's office not a moment after Gail left.

He caught her off guard and she almost jumped out of her silky well moisturized and slightly tanned skin. But that wasn't the worst of it; when she looked at his face and into his eyes she felt like she could just die from shame and the feelings of betrayal she was experiencing. She felt totally and utterly naked as if he could see right through her and instantly knew of the deception and her new role as the office whore.

But she had to overcome somehow; she worked in advertising and could sell anything to anyone so she put on her best 'Evie' and launched into one of her finest performances to date; which actually made her feel far worse because at that very moment she became acutely aware of the fact that there was no longer anything genuine about her relationship with Mike.

She was about to be willfully and intentionally dishonest with Mike and pretend that everything was fine and dandy after being sexually intimate with someone else instead of being open and honest with this wonderful man that she was apparently falling in love with.

But honesty wasn't an option; damage control was the only course of action in her mind. Mike would likely never want to see her again if she told the truth and their personal and professional relationship would surely end in ruins.

As bad as she felt about having to be temporarily ingenuous with Mike where this particular issue was concerned she was prepared to do whatever was necessary to preserve her relationship with him.

Mike continued;

"I came by your apartment last night but you didn't answer the buzzer"

"Sorry, I went out with a friend and got home late... you should have just called me on my cell...perhaps we could have met somewhere"

"That's ok, I thought perhaps it was something like that so I didn't want to bother you; or end up looking like a stalker"

That comment of course was enough to spark thoughts of Tom again.

Mike could see that Eve was distracted and obviously tired but didn't press the issue; it never even occurred to him that she would actually go to Tom's house to give him heck let alone stay for cold spaghetti and hot sex.

"Are you ok Eve? You seem a little distracted this morning"

"I'm fine Mick; late night and I just couldn't get to sleep afterwards; my friend had been having trouble with her marriage and I guess it upset me more than I realized; then I started thinking about the Luzon account and a

million other things; just one of those horrible sleepless nights that happen every now and again"

"I've had them myself Sophie"

"I'm sure you have Vladimir but your sleepless nights are usually caused by blondes and brunettes"

"Hey that's not fair! You've completely left out the red heads!"

They both enjoyed a chuckle; and it couldn't have come at a better time; Mike's charm and inimitable offbeat wit revived her spirits immediately and provided the emotional lift she desperately needed to get through the morning.

When noon finally made an appearance Eve darted out of the building before Mike knew she was gone. But as she hurriedly clicked along the sidewalk her cell phone rang; it was a text from Mike;

"Meet for lunch?"

She texted back; *"Sorry M, grlz lunch today. Talk later"*

He replied *"Have fun"*

It was sweet of Mike to text her but the last thing she needed at that moment was more face time with him; she needed distance and time to talk to her girlfriends about what had happened or she wouldn't make it through the day.

She considered just going home and hiding for the rest of the day but then it occurred to her that it would serve no practical purpose; she would simply end up pacing back and forth talking to herself all afternoon and evening which in turn would result in another completely unnecessary sleepless night and more coffee on her rug.

And there was the distinct possibility of Mike showing up at her place wondering what was wrong; that was the last thing she needed.

When she arrived at the restaurant Lena and Susan were already at a table sitting upright at attention like a couple of cardboard cut-out's at a blowout sale in anticipation of the important secret news that Eve had promised to relay. They waived Eve over to the table the second she appeared inside the front door.

"Hey girls!"

Susan said *"We haven't ordered yet; just got here"*

They made small talk for a few minutes as they perused the menu.

Finally Lena spoke up;

"Ok Eve, enough delay tactics; spill it! What's going on? That mysterious phone call late last night means something is up...what's going on girl?"

"You're right; something is going on and I don't know what to do"

146

"About what? Did something happen to your mom again? Or aren't things going well with Mike? Has he been running around on you already? I knew it; what a jerk!"

"No, nothing like that; Mike hasn't done anything wrong; It's me; I've done something wrong...something really bad!"

Although the girls were genuinely concerned they could also see that this was going to be a particularly juicy gossip session and both leaned in wide eyed to absorb every scintillating detail;

"Tom and I ....ummm...we...you know....."

"Tom and you what? Had dinner, went for a pony ride? Played scrabble in your underwear?....what!"

"I didn't mean for it to happen; it just did; I went to Tom's house to give him shit for breaking Mike's hand and I don't know; we were arguing and the spaghetti was almost ready and he came out of the shower in a towel and his dog was nice and....his body was so...and he sings in the shower and..."

"Evie, please; slow down, you're not making any sense hun"

"Tom....Tom...me....him...we did it!"

"Oh my god....you mean you....."

"Yes...that's what I'm trying to tell you! We slept together....well not slept slept; you know what I mean... we did...it"

Paul Kool

"Can you be more specific in reference to IT?"

"IT...you know..." Eve leaned over the table slightly and whispered the words the girls longed to hear; *"we had sex!"*

"Shut up! You did not!" Susan gasped in horror.

"I'm afraid we did"

"So...how was it?"

"Susan!" Eve said as if to scold her for being so direct and nosey but it didn't work.

"Oh no you don't! You're not going to get off that easy; you call us last night to say you have to talk and we worried all night and all morning and now you say you won't tell us what's going on? No, my dear, you are going to tell us ev-ry-thing!"

"Ok, ok... ummm...I went to Toms to talk; you know, talk about what he did to Mike's hand; we argued and argued and I told him I hated him and he said something mean back and then next thing I know we're kissing right there in the middle of his kitchen"

"That's it?

"I wish it were that simple! In retrospect I should have left right then and there; but we... you know, we got undressed and...ah...."

"Right there in the kitchen?"

"No, no...I mean yes, we did it there...and..."

148

"And what?

"Well…every other room in the house as well" Eve said with a painful look on her face.

"So, how many rooms does he have exactly?"

"Lena!" Susan said using the scolding tactic Eve just tried to use unsuccessfully as if she didn't care to know.

Evie didn't answer that question.

They all just sat there as if in a daze mumbling 'oh my god' over and over while fanning themselves with their napkins not sure what to make of it but unabashedly enjoying every second of it.

Finally Susan spoke up and took another run at it;

"So was it good? I mean compared to Mike…he is supposedly the maestro after all…surely it couldn't have been as good as it is with him"

Evie didn't answer immediately; and actually couldn't even speak because she had suddenly realized something; the sexual romp with Tom was by far the most exciting experience she had ever had.

Not that Mike fell short of his reputation as the maestro; he was a wonderful lover; gentle, sincere, and he knew where every button was and exactly how to push them; he was by all accounts a well-seasoned and highly skilled veteran of the boudoir.

But nonetheless, Evie's temporary silence told its own tale. Of course this set off another few minutes of dramatic 'oh my gods' and napkin fanning.

Finally Eve interjected;

"Let's put it this way; Mike is a great lover and very exciting; Tom is a different person and has a completely different approach to lovemaking"

"He's an animal isn't he; very physical and overpowering...Meeeow!" Lena cooed.

"Yeah, he's something else alright!" Evie said and then just stared off into space for a moment as if savoring the moment...and unwittingly revealing the effect Tom had on her.

They all just sat there for what may have been five minutes just looking at each other and sipping their wine until the server came over to take their lunch orders.

Lena was the first to break the silence;

"But I thought you didn't like him?"

"Oh it goes a lot deeper than just not liking him!.....I can't stand him!"

"So why did you.....oh my god....you're in love with him!"

"That's utterly ridiculous! I don't even know him!"

"Well apparently you do now my dear!"

"Funny, that's what he said...well not quite like that but he said it"

"What?"

"Never mind"

"There are no other options Eve; the only explanation left for hot sex with the sewer guy is that you decided to take our advice and just keep him and his tool belt around for some hot 'repair work' (wriggling her eyebrows and winking) *is that the idea?"*

"No...and what's with the eyebrows...Botox wearing off?"

"Well Eve, this can't be all that bad as I see your wit is still fully functional; so what is it then? It's not like you to just sleep with some guy you apparently don't even like just for the heck of it...or is it?"

"It wasn't just for the heck of it"

"But you said..."

"I know what I said but I don't know what happened; I went there mad and then it just happened; he was different and took me by surprise"

"Different how?"

"I don't know; funny and charming but rude and obnoxious all at the same time. He seemed timid before; this time he was all business; he just took charge and next thing I knew my knees turned to cottage cheese and that was it; I don't know; he just got to me somehow and

151

now I feel terrible...but kind of good too if you know what I mean; I'm sooo confused right now"

"Yeah, I'd be feeling pretty good right now too; but Eve, he sounds like a guy that has nothing to lose"

"What do you mean?"

"He probably figured whatever he did you wouldn't care about him anyway so he just gave up on you and treated you the way he thought you deserved to be treated...and maybe get a little personal satisfaction out of it in the process for all the shitty things you've done to him; but he's obviously still carrying a torch for you"

Eve started to sob as the girls tried to console her; she was obviously in a terrible emotional state.

Once Eve composed herself Susan leaned in and softly said;

"Sweetie; what about Mike?"

"Mike is wonderful; handsome, charming, witty, rich, sexy, a great dresser...who could ask for more? He's everything I could ever wish for in a man...he's exactly what I've been looking for" she said as she dabbed her eyes with her handkerchief.

"But?"

Then Eve suddenly became her old strong self again; she took one big sniffle to mark the end of the sobbing and her nose running; raised her head with her chin up and said;

"But nothing! Tom and I have agreed to just forget this whole ugly incident ever happened...there is no 'but' and there is no us"

"Ugly incident?...doesn't sound ugly to me...it sounds super romantic and sexy" Susan said while putting her hand on Eve's to comfort her and also ensure that Eve paid attention to her next comment;

"I just hope you're being honest with yourself Evelyn because it sounds to me like there is something very real going on between you and Tom"

"Real? Yeah, I really hate him; he took advantage of me!"

"Did he physically force you? Come on Eve, that does not sound like Tom at all"

Eve looked down and conceded;

"You're right; he didn't make me do anything I didn't want to do; actually I kissed him first! This is all my fault...truth is I can't blame him for any of this!"

The girls all gasped after that particular revelation and listened intently as Eve explained;

"Even though we were arguing he didn't do anything to make me feel uncomfortable or threatened; actually now that I think about it I felt perfectly safe the entire time...he has this way of making me feel protected when I'm with him...like he's in charge and whatever happens he'll take care of it; and he has this great dog; a big Labrador Retriever named Eddy...he's so adorable...

and his house was clean and really nice; not exactly the way I'd decorate it but for a guy it was really nice"

Susan could read between the lines and took the opportunity to put in a good word for Tom and to stop Eve from babbling nonsensically;

"He's a nice guy Eve and he's like family to me. Do you really think I'd urge you to go out with him if I had even the slightest suspicion that he was a jerk? He's the big brother I never had; he and I have spent countless hours talking about all sorts of things, in particular you my dear girl! He really likes you despite the way you've treated him"

"The way I've treated him?" Eve said as if shocked and offended by the very notion.

"Eve! It's me; your old friend Sue....snap out of it! I've known you far longer than anyone in this city and I know the real you; the kind hearted small town girl; but sometimes you lose sight of that; I know it's not easy clawing your way up the corporate ladder in a strange city like this; you've done an incredible job and have so much to offer and so much to be proud of but please; just remember that Lena and I love you for the real you; our dear friend; not the smoke and mirrors image you present to the world at work; don't let all this big city glitz and stuff get in the way of 'feeling' and 'loving' and being you; be honest with yourself; because if you aren't then love will pass you by time after time"

*"That was some speech councilor; you should go to law school (*Sue was in fact a junior partner at a downtown law firm)

"Objection! Relevance! Let's stick to the facts that are before the Love Court today shall we?"

"Ok, and good one by the way...nice delivery too"

"Thank you Evie!"

"You're welcome and ok yes there may be just a teensy weensy bit of truth in there somewhere; I guess I have become a little jaded and perhaps a little callous I suppose...but me and Tom? Come on girls he's a sewer worker for god sake"

"And since when does love care what someone's resume looks like? He's a hardworking decent and honest man!"

"And so is Mike; he's so dedicated and so incredibly talented"

"I'm sure he is but he also has one hell of a reputation following him around everywhere he goes and you can't be sure that he'll ever change his ways; sure he's gaga over you right now but there's no guarantee it'll stay that way; he has a pretty colorful history...not to mention a very rich family. He's used to having his way so don't forget that; I hope you haven't confused his lifestyle and all that money and power his family has with love...I must admit it's all like a fairy tale; any girl would kill to be in your predicament; but I guess

this is one of those times in life where it's better to stop thinking and just listen to your heart"

"Maybe so Sue, but I'll tell you one thing; I'm not attracted to Mike because of the money or the power or anything like that; he's just a great guy and we have fun together at work and away from the office...I had no idea his family was rich; it's him I'm interested in not his family"

"I don't envy you; well I do for having two incredible guys to choose from; but not for actually having to make a choice between them"

"My decision is already made; I'm not going to see Tom again...that night was a mistake and it will never happen again!"

"Ok, well it looks like you've resolved this; whatever you decide to do, we're here for you"

"I appreciate that; you guys are good friends and just for the record you're right Sue; Tom is a great guy underneath that rough and tumble exterior of his but I don't think he's the right guy for me; being with him isn't the life I've envisioned for myself and for all I know all he wanted was to have sex with me so he could go and tell his Neanderthal tunnel buddies about it and have a few laughs at my expense...and maybe even have leverage to use against me with Mike"

"Oh you know that's not true Eve; now you're being simply ridiculous! Like I said, he really likes you a lot... it goes well beyond the physical; but if it's not meant to

be then it's not meant to be so let's just leave it at that; we'll support you whatever you decide"

Because of Eve's turbulent emotional state…and three glasses of wine, she didn't even catch onto Susan's discreet and masterful instillation of reverse psychology…not consciously anyway. Freud would have been proud.

"Thanks girls, I really appreciate your support and I'm so sorry I fell apart like that; I feel so much better now. What's done is done; I need to move forward and focus my energy on Mike and me and try and make this up to him somehow, without him realizing it of course"

"And ease your own guilt in the process I suppose?"

"I guess so yes…I have to do something to be able to get past this so I can live with myself somehow; I know it sounds bad but I don't really feel like I have a choice"

Susan looked over at Lena and asked her what she thought about all this to which she replied;

"What the heck do I know? Geezuz, I live alone with two cats and haven't had a date in over a year; I'm hardly qualified to give advice on the subject"

"Lenore! You're a psychotherapist for Christ sake!"

"I hate when you do that by the way"

"What?"

"Call me Lenore"

"It is your given name isn't it?"

"That doesn't make me hate it any less"

"Hmmm...something to do with your childhood perhaps? A repressed incident or trauma?"

"No just a shitty name choice on my parents part; but ok I get it! You want a professional assessment of the situation; why didn't you just say so? I'll still only charge you half the usual rate"

"Funny....now make with the assessment Doc!"

"Ok, here it is in a nutshell; Evie my dear friend and patient de jour, you're beating yourself up for nothing; you and Mike just started seeing one another a few weeks ago and you haven't made any formal commitments, you're not engaged and you're not married. You're still a free agent and well, I guess so is he for that matter so if you insist on worrying about something his 'free agency' would be it; but time will tell; so in my professional opinion as a psychoanalyst holding both the M.D. and Ph.D. designations, my best advice to you at this time is this; GET OVER IT CUPCAKE!

"Lena!" Susan said aghast; *"That was a little insensitive don't you think?"*

"Wait till she gets my bill!"

The girls all laughed but the truth of the matter was that Lena knew full well that what ailed Eve was a simple case of not wanting to repeat the emotional distress of her childhood by marrying a blue collar worker....her father was blue collar.

And it didn't take a doctor to figure it out; Susan had also figured it out years ago and it had been the topic of many a discussion between herself and Lena but neither ever had the heart to actually confront Eve about it.

Lena thought it would be best to support Eve as a friend and let her work through it herself. She was confident that at some point there would be a breakthrough; and hearing the news of the infamous lascivious evening in Queens with terrible Tom was the best news she could have hoped for; it represented progress.

Despite the turmoil and emotional distress Eve was being subjected to at least temporarily, it was the first and much anticipated step towards consciously confronting her issues; the very same ones that were essentially responsible for her not having found the right guy to share her life with.

Lena's professional position on the situation was that Eve was essentially sabotaging herself and her own happiness time after time by choosing men that were obviously not right for her on a variety of levels so she wouldn't have to confront and deal with the issues related to her father...and this 'syndrome' apparently wasn't uncommon; she saw it in her practice quite often.

The crux of the problem was that Eve would unwittingly revert back to simplistic childhood generalizations and confuse them with fact and rationality; for example; all men that work blue collar jobs are bad; professional men are good people; men that don't wear suits are selfish and mean; men that don't have high paying jobs are stupid and immature. Ultimately that line of thinking culminates to perpetuate the mistaken notion that any man that reminds her in the slightest of her father from the way they dress or talk or walk WILL LEAVE HER!

The biggest problem with that line of reasoning was that she placed blame on the wrong person. In reality it was her mother that was the cause of the breakup of her parents for a variety of reasons.

Her father simply couldn't deal with her drinking which had secretly started years before the split not to mention the affairs with strangers she'd met in bars while on one of her many drunken binges.

Eve had somehow blocked all of that out. Essentially her feelings towards her father were completely without merit or rational basis; she also consciously chose to overlook the fact that her father was a hardworking and honest man and sent money each month after leaving; which Eve's mom drank away instantly.

Lena elected to once again keep her thoughts on the subject to herself but did leave Eve with a final thought;

Oh, and I almost forgot; there is of course one other itsy bitsy issue"

"More issues? Oh goody, do tell!" Eve said, chuckling, obviously back in sarcastic-joke mode.

Lena carefully planted her seed;

"Ummm...I don't know if you've noticed babe, but Mike and you are from entirely different social classes... entirely different worlds"

"I did indeed notice that; but thank you for pointing it out! I believe it was the 30 million dollar penthouse and his parent's lil ole country house that happens to be the size of an inner city school that eventually gave it away"

"You know what I mean smarty pants" Lena said as she extended her left arm upwards and wiggled her hand around in the air to signal the server for yet another glass of wine. By this time the girls were all a little tipsy and getting tipsier by the minute.

"Tom called me fancy pants last night while we were arguing just before we...you know...but yes of course I know what you mean; I'm just joshing silly!"

"Well girls, it looks like Miss Evelyn is back among the living!" Lena said while almost knocking over her wine glass while doing her 'here she is ladies and gentlemen' hand gestures as if welcoming a guest on a late night talk show.

"Thank you girls; a toast...to us...friends till the end!" Evie said proudly as she half stood up so she could use the table for balance as she teetered on her heels and raised her glass now more than a little drunk; and apparently convinced she had made the right decision to not see Tom again and to put the whole nasty thing behind her with no guilt attached.

"Hey! I have a great idea; lets ditch work and take this party back to my place; I've got a half dozen bottles of wine lookin to meet three wild ladies" Evie proclaimed.

It took little convincing at that point; Lena and Susan picked their cell phones up off the table and, after punching in a few wrong numbers courtesy of the wine induced state of inebriation, managed to successfully call their assistants and have them cancel their afternoon appointments.

Eve texted Mike to say she was going to spend the rest of the day and evening with the girls and wouldn't be back to the office.

Next stop Chez Evie!

Chapter 11

Six months had passed and everything seemed to be fine.

Evie had managed to stay clear of Tom entirely and she and Mike were continuing to enjoy each other's company both personally and professionally. Mike's hand was out of its cast by then and practically as good as new.

Eve had managed to put her guilt regarding the sordid Tom incident behind her so she could focus all her energy on Mike…and making him love her.

She did everything she could to make it easy for him; she didn't place any demands on him, didn't start the hinting game for an engagement ring, didn't mind if he went out with his friends whenever he liked, never questioned him about what he did when he wasn't with her and was basically the perfect girlfriend at least from his perspective. The word 'overcompensation' comes to mind.

They accepted an invitation to attend Mike's parents' country home in the Hamptons for the long weekend that was fast approaching.

Eve and Mike left directly from the office on the Friday afternoon in hopes of beating the traffic out of the city.

Unfortunately a lot of other people had the same idea; and when I say a lot I of course mean what seemed like half the residents of the city. To say the least it was a long slow drive to the country but it gave them a chance to talk…reeeeally talk!

Mike was surprisingly reserved for the first half hour or so of their journey during which time they had managed to get a whole two blocks away from the office. Eve broke the silence;

"Earth to Vladimir…you're a million miles away; whatcha thinkin about?"

"Apologies Amelia; I'm thinking that if everything goes well this weekend we should consider the notion of perhaps maybe entertaining the possibility of conceivably initiating discussion with regards to a possible cohabitation arrangement…that's basically it"

"You mean live together?"

"No, don't be silly! I'm merely suggesting that we live completely separate lives under the same roof and never so much as even speak to one another or look at one and other as we wander around dressed in bubble-wrap so we don't contaminate each other with our respective boy and girl cooties...of course I mean live together!" Mike said as he chuckled to himself thinking he was being delightfully clever.

"Sounds more like marriage to me!" Eve shot back immediately and performed a fairly respectable air rim shot for a girl, with the 'ba-rrump-bump' sound and everything.

There wasn't a line Mike could come up with that she couldn't counter brilliantly; she was the undisputed reigning champ of their little wit wars and verbal sparring.

Mike learned one important thing about Eve early on in their professional relationship; she was smarter than him...not a lot but just enough to make her interesting as hell.

"Speaking of marriage, do you ever think about it?"

"It depends who's asking, Bruce"

"Seriously Nicole; is it something you think about now and then?"

"I'm a girl Jake; that's ALL we think about buddy boy; with shopping, work and gossip thrown in for good measure as a distraction"

Mike gave Eve the 'come on and be serious' face and she continued;

"Ok ok ok, if we must be serious and not that I want to be on a Friday, I guess the answer would be yes of course I think about marriage and would like very much to get married one day; oh Christ! You're not working up to a marriage proposal here are you because it's way too early for me to start thinking about that sort of thing; I'm not saying no and I'm not saying yes but I need more time to digest it all; so many arrangements to make; invitations, a guest list; bridesmaids dresses; oh my God...and the wedding cake...it's already stressing the shit out of me! Take me home this instant!"

"Whoa...slow down Eve; relax, I'm not working up to a proposal I assure you! I mean yes of course I'm crazy about you and yes, if I was to get married I wouldn't want it to be to anyone but you but I'm not ready either; not that I have any doubts about us but I don't want us to get ahead of ourselves; please don't be mad; it's just really premature...I'm sorry" Mike said feeling guilty and worried about hurting Eve's feelings.

"Mike?"

"Yes Jane"

"GOTCHA!"

"Aha! Actually you didn't get me Frieda because in reality I got you. It was all a ruse to get you to say that stuff"

"Mike?"

"Yes Jessica?"

"Don't embarrass yourself with the backpedalling!"

They both laughed and laughed obviously delighted with the latest round of wit wars for several minutes while taking intermittent sips of the drive-thru coffees that they picked up several miles back. Mike wasn't at all happy about having to resort to drive-thru coffee but there wasn't a Starbucks to be found along that stretch of highway so he had to 'rough it' during the trip.

As they drove along, now well out of the city listening to country music Mike looked over at Eve and said;

"Funny, sexy, beautiful and smarter than me; I think I'm the luckiest guy on the planet!"

"What a sweet thing to say Tom!"

Silence.

"What did you just call me?"

"Lester?"

"No"

"Francesco?"

"No my dear; you called me Tom!"

"So? We just started another round of wit wars didn't we and are in the middle of the name game right now are we not?"

"Yes"

"So what's the problem....run out of names Ricardo?"

Mike pulled off the highway and came to a halt in a rest stop area.

"What's wrong Mike is the car broken? Darn...I don't think we're ever going to get to your folks house at this rate" she said as she casually primped her hair in the vanity mirror.

"You called me Tom!"

Still looking in the mirror and playing with her hair and makeup without missing a beat Eve said *"I'm with you so far Rex; can you elaborate a little on why that's a problem?"*

"Really? Tom? That big galoot that broke my hand?"

"Oh...I see what the problem is; you're jealous you little dickens you!" she said laughing and wagging her finger at him.

Mike wasn't amused.

"Why would you use his name? Are you carrying a torch for him or is there something going on that I haven't been made aware of?"

"Yes, you caught me Hawthorne! Sewer guy and I have been having a torrid love affair for years but he refuses to leave his bedridden six hundred pound wife but we're exploring ways to kill her for the insurance money; we put a deposit on a forklift and everything"

"Eve!" Mike snapped, not angry but insistent on hearing a serious explanation.

But Eve was still 'insistent' on playing her game and making light of the situation;

"Okay, ok, I'm sorry! That was all a lie! The shocking truth is that I NEEDED A QUICK NAME FOR THE GAME AND Tom JUST POPPED INTO MY HEAD SO I BLURTED IT OUT...I'm so ashamed but all I can say in my defense is that ITS JUST A GODDAMN NAME SO GET OVER IT NANCY!" Eve said in a joking tone with her voice slightly elevated to emphasize her point.

"I don't know...sounded a lot like a Freudian slip to me"

"That's all very interesting Sigmund but I assure you that the only slip around here is this one mister" Eve said as she pulled up the hem of her skirt still in her office attire and proceeded to turn the discussion into a love game;

"So how's this for a slip Dr. Freud; isn't it pretty?"

"Most definitely Lana!"

"Would you like to touch it with those big strong hands of yours Dr.?...it's so very soft...don't be shy now" she said in a southern drawl for effect as she took his hand and placed it on her thigh over the lacey portion of her slip;

"So what do you think Siggy? Doesn't that feel nice?"

He began to feel the silk slip and was becoming quite aroused. She threw in a couple of 'oohs' and 'ahs' and I believe possibly one 'oh baby' as he played with the hem of the slip knowing full well that she had him under her control;

"So what does a girl have to do to convince her charming, insanely jealous and oh so sexy man that she wants him and only him and no one else could ever compare?"

She was playing the maestro like a violin and the best response he could come up with, considering of course the fact that there was no blood left in his head because it had heard there was a party in his pants and had left his brain to attend, was;

"...nice nylons too...your legs are so sexy my dear"

"You've been ogling them since I got in the car you naughty boy; I wore these nylons just for you; I think you should satisfy your curiosity and just touch them; would you like that?"

"oh yeah; mmmm...nice" he grunted as he ran his hand up and down her silken thigh for a couple of minutes completely fixated on them like a lobotomy patient; and then leaned in to kiss her.

She liked the way his hand felt as it moved back and forth on the inside of her thigh over the silky nylon that adorned her soft legs.

As their lips touched, Eve suddenly remembered a comment her mother once made when she was young as she watched her mom getting dressed for one of her notorious dates;

"I'll let you in on a little secret child; men can't resist a shapely pair of legs in nylons; makes em bat shit crazy! It's a fact of nature! When you want something from a man you make sure you're wearing nylons and you'll get your way nine times outta ten kid!"

Interesting yes and it appeared to be true! Mike was so enthralled by the sight and feel of Eve's beautiful legs in sheer nylons that his trousers started looking like the 'Big Top' tent at the circus.

He wanted to make love right there in the Tiny Mercedes but Eve suggested they get out and enjoy the wildlife in the adjoining woods. The maestro concurred; I mean why not? He had already pitched a tent!

Once they had finished enjoying nature in all its glory in the adjoining woods…from every conceivable angle and position known to man; and had sufficiently composed themselves, they drove off on their merry way to the Hamptons apparently quite satisfied.

Mike was satisfied with his performance as leading man in "Bambi does the ad exec" and conversely young Evelyn was more than happy with her own performance because in reality that WAS a Freudian slip earlier and Mike was correct in identifying it as such. She had Tom on her mind once again and got caught.

But quick thinking and a little nylon leg seemed to induce the appropriate amount of distraction to give Mike a permanent case of amnesia where the topic was concerned and a pretty respectable painful boner as well.

Not that she didn't enjoy making love with Mike; there was nothing ingenuous in that respect; it just seemed like the appropriate and perhaps advantageous time to enjoy it once again.

She managed to maintain a demure relaxed demeanor for the remainder of the trip despite being quite aware of the fact that she had once again not only lied to Mike but had willfully manipulated him.

Until then she had managed to think about Tom secretly, often fantasizing about that evening at his place; usually late at night when in bed alone and Mike wasn't around.

Typically she would banish thoughts of Tom immediately after indulging in one of her fantasies vowing to never so much as think of him again but it was obvious that those thoughts were now beginning to develop a mind of their own and announce their presence at the most inopportune moments.

But Eve was convinced she could handle it and reasoned away the fantasies as a product of boredom or something equally as benign…and silly. In reality her whole line of reasoning was silly yet she persisted in her denial completely convinced that Mike was the right man for her.

"Hey Buffy, I have an idea; actually the same one I tried to tell you about earlier when we got distracted with the wedding gag;…and the incredible forest sex;

*thank you for that by the way; most enjoyable indeed!
But...ummm...we didn't finish our discussion regarding
cohabitation"*

*"Oh Biff...golly...gee willikers... cohabitation sounds
really neato-keen but SERIOUSLY MICHAEL are you
kidding? You're The Maestro for Christ sake! I mean
how do you go from that to being a one woman man in
the blink of an eye? Isn't there some kind of withdrawal
or post-traumatic stress thing that happens there?"*

*"Yes actually; you're quite correct Conchita! One of the
side effects entails getting an acute uncontrollable and
I might add particularly robust and formidably sized
aching super-freak boner for you and your breathtaking
legs and stockings at the drop of a hat...like now for
example"* he said pointing down towards his lap.

Eve looked down and it was pretty obvious that
construction had already begun on another big top tent.
She leaned down closer to his lap and addressed the
little worker men in his pants as well as his penis which
was kind enough to stand up and listen intently;

*"I'm flattered I really am but if Mike and I can't finish
our discussion like adults with no more horseplay it's
going to get awfully lonely in that tent this weekend!"*
she said while wagging her finger at his crotch.

That seemed to rectify the acute case of topic avoidance
Mike was experiencing but surprisingly didn't affect
the quality of his relentless boner one bit;

*"Evelyn my dear I have no reservations whatsoever
about living with you; neither do the little men in my*

pants; and I speak for all of us when I say that we aren't the slightest bit interested in seeing anyone but you under the big top...besides, they've gotten quite attached to you"

"So no reservations whatsoever and no one but me gets a free pass to Mike's Magnificent Big Top?

"Correct!"

"So I guess we're moving in together then"

"I guess we are"

"Yup"

"Uh huh"

"Definitely"

"I want you so badly right now Lana!"

"Me too! Drive faster Felix!"

Chapter 12

They arrived at the country estate forty minutes later and made a b-line straight for Evie's room. Mike jumped right onto the bed and lay there on his back apparently proud of the construction that was still going on inside his pants; the big top was starting to look more like a shopping mall or inflatable rubber raft with each passing second.

Eve took note and conversely also took the opportunity to take their little love game to new heights;

"Hey Horatio, I don't know about you but I'm feeling a little dirty after that long drive!"

Eve unzipped her snug fitting pencil skirt and slid it down her thighs and let it fall to the floor there at the foot of the bed as Mike urged his construction supervisor to get his crew to work faster on the tent; the black slip came off next and ended up high atop the pinnacle of the Big Top.

There she stood in nothing but hellishly high heels and sexy sheer black pantyhose slowly unbuttoning her blouse as the sunlight fell upon her dangerously slippery silky curves through the huge bedroom window looking out over the surrounding grounds and woods.

She carefully placed her blouse on the bed, kicked off her high heels and walked off towards the bathroom seductively; he inhaled her perfume as he followed apparently defying the laws of gravity by being able to walk upright with that monstrous protrusion in his pants.

She unhooked her bra and tossed it over her shoulder with expert precision hitting Mike squarely in the face as he followed the trail desperately pulling off his own clothes as if engulfed in flames.

Once in the enormous bathroom, Mike, totally naked at that point dropped to his knees, reached up and gently started to roll down Evie's pantyhose kissing her magnificently curvaceous hips, thighs, knees, and then ankles while running his hands gently up and down her legs and caressing her fanny.

She lifted one foot at a time and he gently pulled of her nylons, stood up and handed them to her because quite frankly he didn't have any idea what to do with them or where he was supposed to put them; he felt a little awkward holding them...but it was exciting as hell.

Eve alleviated his anxiety and draped the stockings around his neck, pulled him into the shower stall, turned on the water, and they... proceeded to rid themselves of their...dirt?

Once showered and dressed and apparently quite proud of their respective performances, the happy couple made their way down the enormous winding staircase regally descending upon the entry hall only to find no one there to greet them which was a bit of a relief as things got noisier than usual in the shower earlier.

Mike pulled out his cell phone and called his mom; she answered immediately.

Apparently his parents were at the stables.

Mike and Eve joined them there a half hour later after a rather hurried yet much needed glass of wine by the fireplace in the Great Room.

"Evie my dear, so nice to see you again" Mikes mom said as she gave Eve a hug upon their arrival at the stables; likewise for Mike senior.

After a little chitchat about the drive and the weather and so forth Betsy said;

"So Eve if memory serves correctly, last time you were here you mentioned that you used to ride; we were just about to go; would you like to join us dear?"

"I would love that, thank you!"

"Hector, please bring the mare for Miss Evie and Michael's horse as well" she shouted to the stable man at the far end of the building, grooming one of what

must have been twenty or more horses they kept there in the stalls.

A few minutes later they were off riding through the ostensibly boundless fields and rolling green hills that comprised the grounds in the brisk sun filled late afternoon air.

Evie felt like she was living in a fairytale.

She forgot all about Tom and just basked in the glory of the moment; there she was riding a horse with the fabulously rich and powerful Dubrow's on their private estate with their handsome successful son Mike, the love of her life right there next to her smiling like the sunshine itself after an incredible round of shower sex.

And then it ground to a screeching halt; literally. As they galloped along in a comfortable half-stride Evie's horse became spooked by something and it threw her right off into the brush just before reaching the stream that ran through the property.

Mike quickly hopped off his horse as he yelled ahead to his parents to return.

They quickly turned tail and raced back to the scene of the mishap only to find Evie standing there in the underbrush covered in burrs and weeds brushing herself off and laughing uncontrollably with Mike looking on in utter amazement.

"I'm ok folks, just a few scratches!"

*"Evie there's blood on your arm, you're cut; we should call Dr. Kline; he's back from Nassau; (*quickly turning to Mike senior for a moment*) I heard they went down with the Patterson's; I thought they didn't like them?"*

"They don't...interesting" Mike senior said.

After relaying the socialite newsflash Betsy turned her attention back to Eve who was in the process of clawing her way out of the bushes still laughing hysterically, pointing at Mike and saying *"you should have seen your face when I popped my head out of the bushes Mick... oh my god...so hilarious!"*

"Well I was concerned for you!" he said in a slightly cross tone of voice; a tone Eve hadn't heard before.

"I'm sorry Mike...I couldn't resist; but wow; that was fun; I haven't done that in a longtime"

"But you're hurt my dear" Betsy interjected; secretly astounded at how resilient Eve was.

"Oh I've fallen off a lot of horses in my day Betsy, believe me; but I haven't met one yet that could keep me from getting back on!" Eve laughed again.

"Oh God!" Betsy screeched!

"No really Betsy, I'm fine!"

"No, don't move Eve! Michael, do something immediately!"

Mike just stood there frozen and petrified as Betsy pointed down. There was a snake slithering past Evie's feet.

Eve looked down in delight and swooped in like a hawk seizing the serpent behind the head and held it up to her face;

"Aha! Gotcha! So you're the little dickens that spooked my horse; Yer a naughty little bugger arentcha!" she said grinning like she had just discovered plutonium.

Mike and his parents couldn't believe what they were seeing; demure and stylish big city gal and ad exec Evie suddenly turned into Annie Oakley right before their very eyes; they all probably wondered when the six shooters and bullwhip were coming out...well... mostly Mike.

"Whatever you do don't bring that ghastly creature anywhere near me...I didn't even know we had those horrible beastly things on the property; I'm going to talk to the groundskeepers about this!" Betsy said, now dismounted and hiding behind her horse.

"Why it's just a lil ole three foot garden snake Betsy, he won't hurt ya...come and pet him, he's beautiful, I'll hold him for ya"

"Not a chance in hell my dear!"

"Really Betsy, come; it's ok, you trust me don't you?"

"Ewww...I don't know" she said hunching her shoulders as if she was freezing and making yucky faces much

like Mike's friend Sebastian. Eve wondered if all rich people made yucky faces.

Betsy, after a little more coaxing from Eve, finally approached and cautiously touched the snake with one finger along its back and then stroked it a few times. She still refused to hold it but it was the first time she had ever touched one and it was an experience she'd likely never forget.

They all decided to head back to the stables. Eve and Mike raced ahead and arrived a few minutes before Mike's parents.

As they arrived Eve spotted Hector halfway down the corridor of the stable building and rode her horse over to him and jumped off;

"This horse doesn't like water does it Hector"

"No maam"

"Does Mrs. Dubrow know that?"

"Yes of course maam"

"Thank you Hector"

Evie walked back to the end of the stable where Mike was waiting.

"Okay buckaroo, lets git some grub!" Evie joked.

She put up a good front pretending to be happy and upbeat but the truth was she knew she had an even bigger problem on her hands than the issue with Tom; Betsy was gunning for her!

That accident by the stream was no accident! Betsy could obviously see that things were getting serious between Eve and Mike so she specifically asked for that horse knowing it didn't like water and that it would buck her when they got near the stream.

Evie considered the possibility that perhaps Betsy even counted upon Eve breaking an arm or a leg which would have conveniently kept her out of action long enough to try and get Abby and Mike together.

Little did Betsy know that Eve suspected something as soon as she was thrown; she knew horses and knew how some, particularly the breed she happened to be riding can be skittish around water unless trained otherwise.

Thankfully the snake served as a convenient misdirection prop keeping Betsy under the delusion that Eve was oblivious to her little game by citing the snake as the cause of the tumble.

So there it was in all its glory! The dreaded social class issue had emerged from the shadows just as Sue predicted it would...and perhaps on some level Eve expected as much.

She elected to keep her concerns about the incident to herself as she and Mike headed back to the house to cleanup for dinner; apparently several friends and family were to attend as well.

As Eve was getting undressed for her shower Mike decided to have a little fun still amazed by her recently unveiled secret persona;

"Hey Annie! Gitcher gun!"

"What in god's name was that supposed to be Senior Sanchez?"

"That was my Wild West impression; sucked didn't it"

"That's an understatement Hershel!"

They both laughed and then Mike took Evie's hand and gently pulled her to sit next to him on the side of the bed;

"You said you were from a small rural town but I had no idea you were so...so...tough; I mean did you see the looks on mom and dad's faces when you stood up and climbed out of those bushes!"

"Their faces? Shit, you should have seen yours! But hey, don't get the wrong idea; just because I grew up in the country doesn't mean that I'm any less a lady; don't forget that buster!"

"Yes maam!"

"That's better! Now kiss me or I'll have to hogtie you!"

Mike happily obliged and gave her a thoughtful gentle kiss.

He loved what was happening; it was like having two beautiful and extraordinary women rolled into one unbelievable body; one demure refined highly educated professional woman and the other a country wildcat, barefoot in blue jeans that can ride horses and play rough and tumble with the boys; he was in heaven.

"Sebastian is here...just noticed his car come up the drive" Mike said now standing in front of the window looking out;

"I'm going to go downstairs and say hello"

"And leave me here all alone? Not a chance bub!"

"Ok...sorry...if you feel that strongly about it; I didn't mean to abandon you my dear"

"Salvatore?"

"Shit, you got me again didn't you!"

"Didn't see that one coming huh? Just kidding; I'm fine so by all means go say hi to your friend and I'll join you shortly"

Off he went.

And off Eve went; straight to the riding satchel tucked under the bed that she was wearing earlier when she fell off the horse, took out the garter snake that she discretely slipped inside it while the others were turning their horses around, snuck into Betsy's bedroom, gently pulled back the covers on her bed, deposited the snake between the sheets and carefully put the covers back as they were.

Then she showered, got dressed and went to join the others downstairs.

She looked absolutely radiant; like a model straight from the pages of a fashion magazine and every eye in the house was on her as she came down the winding staircase to join the sea of guests.

When she touched down at the bottom of the stairs Sessile greeted her with a sincere smile and a glass of white wine;

"You look absolutely amazing Eve!"

"Thank you Sessile, as do you!"

"So here we are for another one of these boring affairs; I'm glad you're here or I'd have no one to talk to"

"But you know everyone"

"Exactly!"

The girls both laughed and went off arm in arm to a quiet corner to chat about clothes and work and so forth.

"Oh Christ! Tell me she didn't do that!"

"What?"

"True to form Betsy has taken it upon herself to invite Abby and her parents; I don't know if Mike told you about her"

"Yes, he did; she's the...how did he put it...'brainless doggie carrying wonder' that his parents want him to marry for no other reason than they are close friends with her parents...is that the one?"

"The very same!"

"My god, you'd think with all that money she'd know how to put a decent outfit together...if that hemline was any shorter that dress would be a top"

"Maybe she thinks Mick will like it?"

"Mike thinks she's gross; reminds him of Paris Hilton; and by the way I love the pet name thing you guys have going...it's so cute!"

"It's just a silly little game we play"

"You guys really do get along well don't you"

"Yes we do; at work and in our personal lives; it's so nice to be with a man that has a great sense of humor"

"I wouldn't know (chuckling*) but anyway...it really wasn't nice of Betsy to try and play Abby and you off against each other"*

"That's fine Sessile; she's certainly entitled to invite whomever she chooses to her home"

"Yes my dear but you don't understand; Betsy is obsessed with seeing the two of them together; it's not even about love...it's business more than anything; kind of a merger between the two families...money at stake, appearances and all that....it's always about money with these people....they try and act like it's not but it is!"

"Why are you telling me this Sessile?"

"Because I like you; you're good for Michael and I also think you and I are going to be good friends...it's so nice having you around"

"That's so sweet of you to say Sessile, thank you for that!"

"But hey, just watch your back girl...well I better go and mingle and say hi to a few people; I'll find you later and see how you're doing"

Unbeknownst to Sessile Eve was more than capable of looking after herself and moreover wasn't the slightest bit shocked by Abby's presence; in fact she fully expected it.

And she also knew that Betsy would be watching her every move trying to gauge her reaction to Abby. This wasn't a problem for Eve; she simply adjusted her thinking accordingly and put on yet another award winning performance; flawless in fact.

Eve walked right over Abby and introduced herself as Mike's girlfriend and the two chatted for a few moments before Eve left her to go outside onto the patio for a smoke.

She came back inside to find Abby tagging along behind Mike and trying to intervene in every conversation he engaged in with the guests during his tour of the room as the music of the jazz trio hired for the occasion echoed throughout the mansion over the voices of the guests.

By all accounts it was a lovely evening but it was no longer magical...it was sterile, contrived and superficial.

Eve felt that the acceptance she had hoped for was simply a delusion and the underhanded trick that Betsy pulled with the horse was in her estimation a dirty and despicable act and it not only hurt her emotionally; it angered her; but what the heck; she had that covered like sheets on a bed!

There were times during the evening that Eve would just go off alone to try and find a quiet place to sit away from all the talking and laughing, glad-handing, drinking and bragging about vacations in the south of France and places Eve had never even heard of and yachts and cars and the stock market and all the rest of it.

It had all suddenly become...for lack of a better descriptor....boring as hell just as Sessile had described it....nothing but one big business meeting with alcohol, food and a band.

And Abby in particular?

Eve was of the opinion that she was absolutely pathetic. She suddenly realized that she didn't even need to put on an act to pretend that she wasn't affected by Abby's presence; she truly wasn't.

Abby if nothing else provided the comic relief to an otherwise lost evening. Eve especially liked watching her scurrying about at Mike's heels desperately trying to get his attention and corner him at every opportunity as Mike did his best to avoid her.

In fact there were times Eve would actually have to cover her mouth because she could barely contain her laughter; Abby was like a spoiled child in need of a good spanking….and Eve would be happy to provide it if necessary.

This was one time where Eve's self-esteem was operating at peak proficiency; she herself could see that Abby wasn't in her league in terms of accomplishments, looks, brains or anything for that matter; but Abby was from a wealthy family well within Mike's family social circle so there was still just a hint of concern.

The evening went wonderfully otherwise; and the screams of horror coming from Betsy's room that night when she climbed into bed more than made it all worthwhile.

Eve and Betsy barely spoke for the remainder of the weekend.

Chapter 13

Needless to say there were no more invitations to the country house in the months that followed and the events of that infamous weekend were never discussed openly.

How could they be? If Betsy was to accuse Eve or relay her suspicions about the snake incident to Mike then Eve might have shared her thoughts about Betsy's choice of horse and the conversation with Hector immediately afterward. It was best to leave it alone.

But Eve reminded herself that none of it even mattered; she didn't care about Mike's family or what they thought. She was in love with Mike and he was in love with her. That was the only thing that mattered; simple as that!

Eve and Sessile started to see more of each other and would meet for lunch every couple of weeks to do some shopping or have dinner or see a show together. Her friendship with Sessile was the only positive thing to come out of meeting Mike's family and friends.

Sessile's family was wealthy as well; nouveau rich, not old money like Sebastian and Mikes families; she was blue collar underneath it all and still shopped at Walmart for her everyday clothes despite the fact that she could literally buy designer clothes by the truckload if she liked.

Her grandfather who was a machinist in a metal fabricating factory apparently developed a mechanical device that revolutionized assembly line work allowing one set of machines to be quickly adapted by simply changing a few parts to produce different sizes of metal cans and containers interchangeably as opposed to having to setup entirely different machines for the variance in size and shape and so forth.

"Boy did I ever have trouble with Sebastian's mom when he and I started going out...sheesh! Those Boston people are so guarded when it comes to who they associate with...she hated me for the longest time; probably still does but puts up with me because she can't get rid of me and I was the only girl from a wealthy family that was willing to date Sebastian so she's stuck with me" Sessile confided during an evening out with Evie.

"So how did you get her off your back?"

"Well I wish I would have done what you did and put a snake or something in her bed; my god you've got gumption girl! I really admire that!"

"Shit...how did you find out about that?"

191

"The usual; Betsy told Mike senior who told Sebastian's dad who told Sebastian who told me"

"How do they know I was responsible for that?"

"They don't; all Betsy said was that she suspected you but didn't want any of it getting back to Mike for his sake as your actions would hurt him deeply"

"What a dramatic little bitch!"

"You don't have to tell me; I've been watching the drama unfold for years now; one thing after another with that woman; and same goes for Sebastian's mom; no wonder they're best friends...I figured it was probably you that pulled the snake gag because Betsy did something shitty to you or annoyed you somehow; but don't worry I haven't said a word to anyone"

"Annoyed doesn't begin to describe it"

"I'm almost afraid to ask but I guess I am"

"That bitch deliberately gave me a horse to ride that is afraid of water and when we were near the creek which she led us straight to by the way, it threw me off"

"Oh my god; are you ok?"

"Perfectly fine; I grew up on horses and have been thrown further and harder many times so that's not even the issue...it's the sneakiness that really bugs me"

"Not that I doubt a word of what you are saying Eve but how do you know she deliberately gave you that horse?"

"Simple; she asked for it and Hector brought it; oh and it gets better; as soon as we got back to the stables after our lovely ride I discretely asked Hector if the horse I was riding was afraid of water"

"And...was it?"

"Uh huh!...and then I specifically asked if Betsy was aware of that and he said yes"

"wow...that's actually kind of scary when you think about it; I mean you could have broken an arm or leg or even been killed...that would make her like a murderer or something...that's a bit of a stretch...even for her"

"Mike still doesn't know anything about this does he"

"Not that I know of but rest assured he will; Sebastian is like his personal little soldier and reports everything to him so I'd fully expect it's just a matter of time before Mike confronts you"

"That's fine, let him!"

"What are you going to tell him?

"The truth!"

They left it at that for the moment.

As predicted Sebastian told Mike and he confronted Eve over dinner a few nights later at her place;

"Hey Barbara, remember that night at my parents place in the country when my mom started screaming like a banshee in the middle of the night and my dad pulled a little garter snake out of the bed and my mom had to

switch rooms in case there were more and as a result has now sent the entire landscaping crew out onto the grounds for a daily snake hunt and kill and will probably be scarred for life by the incident?"

"Pass the wine please"

"Here you go; so do you?"

"Vaguely"

"And did you have anything to do with that?"

"You betcha! Yeah, I put the snake in her bed...I could hardly keep from laughing when she started hollering like the house was on fire in the middle of the night; geez, took long enough; for a while there I thought maybe the snake had crawled off somewhere else and killed the whole gag"

Mike just sat there with a blank look on his face saying nothing.

"So are you going to ask me why I did it or does it even matter?"

"Oh please by all means; enlighten me Eve!"

"Your dear mother set me up to fall off that horse; how's that for starters?"

"Not bad if it were true"

"You were right there next to me at the stables when she told Hector to bring me the mare correct?"

"Uh huh"

"That mare was frightened of water; you didn't know it and your dad didn't know it but mommy dearest sure as hell did!"

"How do you know that?"

"Because I asked hector that's how!"

"And he confirmed this?"

"He sure did sweet cakes!...but I knew it was her from the second I was thrown...I know horses...I grew up with them"

"Oh so you were lying when you gave the snake shit in front of everyone; it was just an act?"

"I think you're missing the point here Carlos"

"Which is?...and please stop playing around and treat this issue with the respect and consideration it deserves...this is a very serious accusation"

"Whatever! The issue is this Michael; your mom knew that horse was afraid of water and deliberately gave it to me to ride knowing it might throw me off by the creek; simple as that! She obviously doesn't like me and wants me out of the picture so you and what's her name with the stupid little dog can be together!"

"Ok, so let me try and understand this; so you think my mother is some evil creature that deliberately tried to physically harm you to get you out of the way?"

"Bingo bub! I knew this would happen sooner or later"

"Oh Eve please stop; you sound delusional; this is all just ridiculous; my mother is a warm and loving woman...a saint... and would never even think of doing something like that to anyone. I'm really shocked at your behavior Eve and to be honest I don't know if I can continue with someone so...so...DELIGHTFULLY CLEVER AND GUTSY AND SO INCREDIBLY HOT! GOTCHA, GOTCHA, GOTCHA, AND TRIPLE GOTCHA EPONENTIALLY!!"

He really did get her good that time. It was indeed the ultimate 'gotcha' and completely caught Eve off guard.

"Roderick! You nasty boy you!! I'm shocked and appalled at the trickery and deceit and am so incredibly horny right now I can't even begin to describe it...go have a shower and when you come out you'll find a hot secretary in stockings, heels and a skirt so tight you may not be able to pull it off waiting for you with a glass of wine in the living room...and Benito?"

"Yes Margaret"

"Don't bother putting on any clothes"

Mike and his magic portable tent made a b-line for the bathroom and emerged ten minutes later with a boner the size of the Hindenburg to find Eve sitting with the lights low and jazz playing softly on the stereo with her hair up and glasses on in full secretarial garb as promised.

She had once again proven that she was indeed the sexiest woman Mike had ever seen in his life. And he demonstrated that; over and over and over again on every piece of furniture in the tiny apartment.

Problem solved! It actually went much better than Eve had anticipated.

When they were finished they ended up on their backs huffing and puffing staring up at the ceiling on the living room floor.

"So you're not mad about your mom?"

"Naw, it was good for her; she's gotten really stuck-up over the last few years; don't get me wrong; she's my mom and I love her dearly but sometimes she can be pretty cold and controlling and downright mean; serves her right as far as I'm concerned...but still I'm not so sure she'd actually try and physically hurt you or anyone but I'm going to discuss it with her this weekend; I have to pop by for an hour or two; dad said he wanted to talk to me about something"

"So what do you think it could be?"

"Probably threats; he's going to give me the 'she's not from our world' speech and tell me to drop you like a hot potato or I'll be cut off from any money and will have to move out of the condo"

"Oh shit! I'm so sorry; I guess I was hoping it wouldn't come to that...so what are you going to do if he threatens you with that stuff?"

"Drop you like a hot potato...I'm even considering having you murdered so the topic never comes up again"

"But seriously Leopold, kidding aside; this could be the end for us; you know that right?"

"Eve I was just kidding...this is most certainly not the end, it's just the beginning whether they are onboard or not"

"That's nice in theory Sir Fuckalot but it still leaves an insurmountable problem for us to deal with"

"And what's that?"

"Gee I don't know Mike; the fact that if you stay with me and don't marry the doggy whisperer you get evicted, disowned by your family and probably disinherited"

"So how is that a problem?"

"C'mon Michael you can't do that; I won't let you do that!"

"Why? Are you saying that I'm no longer appealing to you without my family's money? Wow...I didn't see that coming!" Mike sat down and covered his face with his hands to add a little drama.

"Are you fucking kidding me Melvin? I don't give a shit about your money; you know damn well I didn't even know you or your family even had any and furthermore all that stuff bores the shit out of me and I could care less"

"Eve?"

"Oh you sonovabitch!....you got me again didn't you!"

"Yes ladies and gentlemen that's two; count em; two huge monstrous consecutive 'gotchas' in one night!"

"Michael I worry about you sometime...I hope you're not developing a 'gotcha' addiction...I read an article about it last week....pretty serious stuff"

"Nice recovery Helen"

"Thank you"

Eve snuggled up next to Mike;

"But hey, seriously, what are we gonna do baby?"

"Maybe we're overreacting a little; to be honest I really don't know what father wants to talk to me about; it could be something quite unrelated but I guess it doesn't even matter; sooner or later he'll get around to it anyway; it may as well be now so we can get it over with all at once"

"So what are you going to tell him?"

"The truth of course; that I love you and fully intend to spend the rest of my life with you; for richer or poorer! If they don't like it then fuck em!"

"Oh my god Beauregard....such language...I've never seen you so aggressive and assertive; I like it Tiger!

"So glad darling; but look, they don't matter; you matter and I matter; we both have great jobs and make a pretty

respectable living between the two of us; I don't imagine we'd have too much trouble getting by financially"

"I'm not worried about that at all; that's not the issue; but really Michael, they're your family; you can't just walk away from them like that"

"Watch me! And by the way there is one other matter I'd like to discuss with you"

Mike dropped to one knee and pulled a tiny box out of the pocket of his sport coat and opened it.

"Marry me Evelyn!"

"Oh Mike! I need some time to think; I love you I really do but how can I just stand by and watch you walk out of your family's life? Money or not it's just not the right thing to do...they are your flesh and blood and that counts for something; we have to work that out somehow"

"So is it better to walk away from us? Not an option! We're meant to be together Eve; fate brought us together and will keep us together no matter what happens; and besides, I can't just live my entire life doing what my parents want me to do and be what they want me to be; and them telling me who I can or can't marry is just utterly absurd and I won't stand for it!"

"Well then I guess there's nothing else to say except; WELCOME TO POVERTY BABY!"

Chapter 14

Mike went to speak to his father that Saturday afternoon and returned to Evie's apartment later that evening.

He found Eve sitting at the kitchen table tapping her fingers nervously, eager to hear about what happened;

"Gee, a call at some point would have been nice Michael; I tried to call you twice but it went to message and I have been pulling my hair out all evening wondering how it went and worrying if you were ok"

"Apologies my dear! Well I'm not sure how it went to be honest; I told them we are getting married whether they like it or not!"

"And?"

"And there is someone in the hall that wants to speak to you"

A thousand things went through Eve's mind at that moment; first and foremost that it was Tom and he had told Mike everything.

Mike went over and opened the door; Betsy walked in.

Eve was glad; not only because it wasn't Tom but she had several things she wanted to say to Betsy and this was the perfect opportunity to blow off some more steam regarding the horse incident and the social circle issue.

"So I gather you came to finish the job and threaten me and tell me Mike will be disowned and all the rest of it if he marries me or so much as sees me again; for the record I tried to talk him out of this; but we love each other; I don't know what else to say so you can keep your money and your fancy lifestyle; I'm not interested in any of it; Mike and I love each other and nothing is going to keep us apart!"

"Are you going to offer an old lady a seat my dear or shall I collapse from exhaustion right here on your floor?"

"I'm sorry Betsy, I'm terribly upset as you can see!"

"Yes, I can see that; a glass of wine would be lovely if you don't mind dear"

"Of course, anything else?....maybe some lunch with some rat poison in it?"

Eve delivered the wine as requested and continued with her attack;

"My god Betsy, how could you do something like that? I could have been hurt or even killed falling off that horse!"

"Are you quite finished my dear?"

"For now"

"Lovely! First of all my dear young lady; the horse that Hector brought was NOT the mare I requested; we have six mares of the same breed; I meant the mother but for some reason Hector brought you the youngest one that wasn't water trained yet; I suppose I should have asked for her by name so that was my mistake. Nonetheless, I asked him about it and he said he assumed that you hadn't ridden and didn't anticipate the horse going as far as the creek, perhaps just a short ride near the stables; the other five mares were in the process of being groomed at the time so he simply brought the one that was available and didn't think it would matter; and we didn't inform him of where we intended to ride so naturally no one anticipated the unfortunate events that ensued; he sends his most sincere apologies for the mix up...and I owe you an apology as well; I should have communicated our intentions regarding the ride and so forth to Hector more clearly; of course there is the matter of a slight language barrier that didn't help matters either...so unfortunately this was simply a case of miscommunication and nothing else I assure you!"

Eve sat down and after a minute of silence finally spoke;

"Oh my God! I feel like such an idiot; I didn't want to believe that you'd do something like that but when I asked Hector if you knew about the horse being skittish around water I guess my imagination just took over and assumed you were guilty without even considering the possibility of a mix up....I am so very sorry I doubted you Betsy; And when Abby showed up at the party just hours after my fall from the horse I just assumed you made a point of inviting her to make me feel even more uncomfortable"

Betsy laughed;

"My dear....I didn't invite Abby! I invited her parents; she was supposedly going away for a couple of weeks to Aruba with friends but for some reason her plans changed and they called at the last minute and asked if she could tag along; she usually avoids these functions so I was rather surprised that she even wanted to attend but conversely it's no secret that she is carrying a torch for Mike so I suppose she wanted to get a good look at you but regardless, what was I to do? Turn her away? Her parents are old and dear friends of ours and to be perfectly honest, after seeing how you handle yourself on a horse I didn't think you'd have much trouble taming young Miss Abby if she got out of line...really my dear!"

"Yes I suppose you're right; but certainly her parents are going to be quite upset when they hear that Mike and I are going to be married"

"Naturally they're going to be very disappointed that Mike has found love with someone other than their daughter but I'm sure they will understand that Mike's happiness is the issue here; I'm ashamed to admit it but I myself overlooked that fact for a while; all of this hoopla has made me realize how easy it is to forget what is truly important in life"

"Oh crappers Betsy, I'm so embarrassed I could just die!"

"Well don't do that my dear; we have a wedding to plan"

"You mean you're actually ok with this?"

"Ok?....my dear girl I'm simply delighted! I knew you were the one for Michael the first second we met... you're strong...he needs someone like you to keep him in line and remind him of what's important in life...much the way you have reminded me"

Eve started to cry with happiness and embarrassment and hugged Betsy;

"I'm so sorry Betsy....the snake....I made assumptions and overreacted...god I don't know why I do that sometimes"

"Now now dear; don't be too hard on yourself; I suspect I might have done something similar if I was in your position; and truth be told I've pulled more than a couple of shall we say questionable stunts in my time... you remind me a little of myself when I was your age"

"So the social circle business isn't an issue?"

"Not for me...it may be an issue for some people but I suppose they'll just have to deal with it; but I can honestly say that everyone that has met you has found you to be simply enchanting regardless of where you come from....the look on Michaels face when you walk into the room tells all"

*"And Mikes dad? Is he ok with this? No, but he will be! Leave it to me; I know how to handle that stubborn old coot! Sometimes that man just needs a good kick in the pants! What matters is Michaels happiness...nothing else!....and my dear you are what makes him happy so as far as I'm concerned there is little to discuss in this regard. (*Handing Eve the empty wine glass and while checking a message on her phone*) Ah ha, Waddington has arrived to take me home; I'll leave you two lovebirds to your evening!"*

"Thank you so much Betsy...I can't tell you how much this means to me"

"No! Thank YOU my dear; Mike couldn't have found a better person to share his life with...any girl that can get thrown from a horse and then laugh and get right back on and then have the gumption to pull that snake stunt is ok in my book! You've got hutzpah my dear and I admire that! But enough of this for now; let's move onto new horizons; why don't we have lunch next week and start talking about the wedding...I'll call you....but do not bring any snakes, agreed?"

"Agreed!"

"And Evie"

"Yes Betsy"

"Everything is going to be just fine; welcome to the family my dear!"

Betsy gave both Eve and Mike a big hug and left. They were both ecstatic!

"Wow senior Hernandez....I didn't see that one coming!" Eve said while pouring her and Mike a glass of wine and curling up on the sofa while basking in the afterglow of this monumental victory.

"I'm shocked as well Miranda...I really didn't think she would do that; I fully expected my father to give me the social circle speech though.... all he wanted was to discuss my taking on a position in the family business again; one of his senior VP's is retiring and he wants me to take over....I told him I'd consider it and I also told him about our plans"

"And how did he react?"

"Well...he didn't actually; he just suggested we stick to the business at hand for the moment and discuss the marriage issue at another time...it think 'reschedule' was the word he used"

"But wait a minute, so how did your mom find out?"

"I caught up with her in the kitchen before leaving and told her about our decision; she didn't react much either....just an 'oh I see' and not much else; so I left and started driving back here thinking they either didn't

take it seriously or were devising some plot to extricate me from the situation as if I am unable to think for myself or something; but I couldn't have been more wrong obviously; I was a couple of miles from the house when she called and asked me to return to pick her up; all she would tell me was that she needed to speak to you in person and not to call you ahead of time or answer if you call as you might not want to see her; that's all I knew...and here we are"

"And so we are"

"Uh huh"

"Yes indeed!"

"You betcha!"

"Sex?"

"Splendid idea!"

Despite all the worry and frustration over Betsy and the dreaded social circle issue things were finally on track. Eve had managed to gain acceptance from Mike's family by simply being herself...sort of.

The very next day Eve summoned Sessile to a popular downtown eatery for lunch so she could tell her the good news;

"Oh my god! I heard....this is so wonderful; congratulations!"

"Gee, nothing like spoiling a surprise is there Sess!"

"Oh shoot....I'm sorry..."

"No, not you Sessile....I think we're going to have to blame Mick and Sebastian for this one; I told him to not say anything to Sebastian until I had a chance to tell you personally first"

"It's always nice to have a man around to blame isn't it?"

"Ya got that right!"

The girls had a little chuckle and Eve suddenly realized that she had just uttered the phrase she herself detested more than anything; but she had no idea why it fell out and wasn't about to start thinking about it.

Sessile continued;

"I have to confess something Eve; I feel a little guilty for saying those things about Sebastian's mom and Mike's mom; I think I was being a little harsh; yes they are dramatic little snobs and yes, they can be a little underhanded at times but they aren't quite as horrible as I made them out to be and I'm sorry if I gave you the wrong impression"

"Ok...fess up sister! They got to you didn't they; did they use electroshock to get you to change your story?"

"Unfortunately things never get that exciting when it comes to Mike or Sebastian's family's and it's no secret that Sebastian's mom and I have had our fair share of battles over the years but we manage to coexist somehow; but I did get a visit from Betsy"

"Aha! Here it comes....I knew this was too good to be true; what did she want you to do, spy or help her in an elaborate murder plot to get rid of me?"

Sessile laughed;

"Hardly! All she wanted was to make sure that I help make you feel comfortable and like part of the family... which you obviously will soon be; she was worried that because of the misunderstanding you guys had you might still feel a little apprehensive about things; she doesn't want that"

"That's it?"

"Ah no, she also told me how fond of you she is; I think she used the word hutzpah more than once in fact"

"You know her fairly well; do you believe her?"

"Yes, I've known her for a longtime...I can tell when she's being a little less than forthcoming and this wasn't the case; she was being quite genuine and sincere so yes, I do believe her; I just wish that was the case with Sebastian's mom and I; we basically go through the motions; she's never liked me and never will but you're very lucky Eve, Betsy is really looking forward to having you as her daughter in law"

"Wow; I hope so; I mean I really want to believe but there's still just a tiny sliver of mistrust in the back of my mind that won't go away but perhaps in time it'll work itself out"

"I hope so Eve; you're going to have a fabulous life; and I hope you're going to join some of my girlfriends and me for our social club meetings and functions; we'd love to have you!"

"Well I really appreciate that Sessile; thank you so much, I'd love to!"

"Anyway my dear, new topic; so the wedding.....how are things going?"

"Betsy and I had lunch a few days ago and started jotting a few things down and slowly getting things organized and underway; I think we're going to have the ceremony and reception all out at the country estate..."

"Oh that would be lovely; did you set a date yet?"

"Not yet; we're just in the initial stages of everything; it doesn't make any difference to me when it is; a week, a month...whatever; Betsy is handling it so whatever works for her is fine with me...she's talking about inviting three hundred of her closest friends...shit, I don't think I've even met three hundred people in my entire life let alone have three hundred friends...this whole thing is kind of surreal to me"

"Well I guess that's part of the reason she wanted me to help you with the adjustment; but don't get me wrong; this isn't one of those 'keep your friends close and your enemies closer' kind of things; you and I had already struck up a friendship before she ever said a word to me about you one way or the other; if there's one person you can trust 100% in all this it's me; and I hope you believe that"

211

"Geez, I don't know Sess; you better be telling the truth or you might find a snake in your bed"

The girls both laughed as Eve continued;

"But seriously; as far as a wedding date goes it's probably safe to assume that it'll be in about three months from now or so; obviously Betsy has a big job ahead of herself getting the guest list sorted out...all I have is my mom to invite and a few close friends"

"Well, if there's anything I can do to help out just let me know; I can arrange a band and the food and all that stuff; I have an amazing caterer"

"I'd love to have you involved but you know that if you go ahead and do something without clearing it with Bets you might land in hot water"

"Actually, you're right! I'm going to call her and offer my services; I'm sure she wants to play queen bee on this along with Sebastian's mom so I'm not going to tangle with the like of those two piranhas....ooops... my bad!"

The girls both broke out in laughter; neither one willing to touch that last comment with a ten foot pole. After lunch the girls went their separate ways; Eve back to the office and Sessile to go talk with Mike's mom to see if she could help with the wedding.

Things were finally going well for Eve; she had found the man of her dreams, had been officially welcomed into the family by the matriarch and was about to have a fairytale wedding... and a fairytale life.

Despite all this she couldn't figure out why she suddenly found herself standing at Tom's door in Queens at eight o'clock on a Tuesday night.

She just stood there without knocking or calling out and lit a cigarette as she stared at the door expecting Eddy to start barking; she assumed he would have heard the click of the lighter or sensed her there but nothing.

She remained still just taking one slow drag of the cigarette, exhaling and slowly taking another drag and exhaling while fixated on the door for no seemingly apparent reason.

When the cigarette burned to the end she dropped it to the ground in front of Tom's door and extinguished it with the sole of her tennis shoe, turned, and left; she didn't get burned that time.

A dozen things went through her head; perhaps Tom had moved because he got wind of the marriage news and it hurt him deeply or perhaps he had gotten hurt at work and was in the hospital and a friend was taking care of Eddy; she had to find out what was going on and at least offer to help look after Eddy.

But then she considered just staying out of it and leaving well enough alone.

She started her car scolding herself for even going to Tom's again particularly when she had no idea what she was doing there in the first place. But as she drove down the street she did decide to at least call Sue and see if she knew anything about Tom's apparent disappearance.

She pulled into the parking lot at the park to make the call and perhaps take a walk to clear her head; pulled out her cigarettes and her cell phone and as usual, Tom had appeared as if from out of nowhere when she least expected to see him.

No wonder he wasn't home; she had completely forgotten that it was time for Eddy's nightly walk and romp in the park; and there they were…right there… not fifty feet from Eve's car in plain view.

She didn't get out; she just sat there watching as Tom ran back and forth while Eddy jumped up on him as they chased each other back and forth on the lawn before finally falling to the ground to continue their wrestling match.

She smiled and then she cried.

The tears fell and fell as if with no end…she wanted so badly to be with them and share the moment but she didn't know why.

After a while she finally managed to compose herself and looked over one last time as she was about to drive away; Tom looked up and their eyes met for one brief second.

He signaled to her.

She drove away with tears in her eyes.

Chapter 15

Eve knew perfectly well that Tom had seen her there in her car with tears in her eyes but since she hadn't heard from him in two weeks she assumed he didn't care about her anymore…and she couldn't blame him a bit as she herself realized that she had treated him badly.

The next night he was ringing her buzzer; she answered it.

"Open up fancy pants, I wanna talk to you!"

"Oh Tom please go away!"

"You don't want me to go away"

"And why is that?"

"Because you know damn well we've got some talkin to do….now hurry up for Christ sake I gotta take a frikin piss real bad"

She buzzed him in and he was in her suite moments later relieving his bladder in her bathroom.

When he came out she was seated on the couch sipping on a bottle of cold beer;

"So let me guess, you were passing by and you had to pee really bad and you decided to just come up here on the off chance that I'd let you use my bathroom?"

"Got more beer?"

"Yup...bottom shelf of the fridge, right side"

Tom went to retrieve his beer and sat down across from Eve on the sofa.

"Nice little place you've got here"

"Thank you"

"So ya wanna tell me what the hell you were doing the other night spying on me in the park?"

"I wasn't spying on you you twit!"

"Twit?...wow, another witty dig from your archive of outdated golden oldie sayings huh? You really need to update your slag files fancy pants...that's as bad as that other thing you said when you showed up at my door to fight Nancy's battles for him"

"Mike"

"What?"

"His name is Mike!"

"Mike, Nancy, whatever!"

"So what do you want Tom?"

"I think the question is what do you want?"

"What does that mean?"

"It means my neighbor said there was a girl that looked like a model standing at my door smoking cigarettes for about a half hour before driving away...you're the only one I know that fits that description...who the hell else would it have been?"

"Maybe it was one of those streetwalkers you like to date"

"I don't date streetwalkers"

"Please! Tell me that Samantha wasn't some sleazy waitress at a strip club or a pole dancer or something equally as degrading and horrid"

"Samantha happens to be a police officer in Brooklyn; and the only reason you didn't get charged with assault after that beer incident is because I talked her out of it"

"Oh shit!...ummm...thank you for that"

"Yeah, oh shit is right! Boy you really do have a talent for jumping to conclusions and summing up people based on nothing don't you!"

"Actually, you know something? You are absolutely right about that and I apologize"

"I'm sorry; I think my ears just went on the fritz; did you just apologize? What's the catch?"

"No catch Tom"

Eve broke down and started to cry.

"Whoa...fancy pants...what's going on? Okay, okay, time out! Let's put away our swords for a while; whaddaya say?...Truce?"

He went to the kitchen and retrieved a box of tissues and handed it to Eve and proceeded to mix them both a couple of double manhattans on the rocks. They needed something far stronger than beer to help navigate the discussion that he sensed was about to take place.

"Okay, please tell me what the fuck is going on with you; did...Mike...cheat on you already or did his fancy family find out you're just a country girl and cut you out of the equation or something?"

"Oh you'd like that wouldn't you! No he didn't cheat on me and his parents don't care where I come from...he asked me to marry him"

Tom just said *"oh, I see"* and walked over to the window to look outside and conceal the fact that he could feel some tears welling up. He was genuinely hurt and disappointed. Not just by the fact that Eve was going to marry Mike but because he didn't think it was the kind of life that would make her happy...it mattered to him.

He secretly composed himself and came back to sit next to her on the sofa;

"So *this is what you want Eve?"*

*"Yes, no, I guess; I don't know what I want anymore;
I should be happy but I'm just miserable; I don't know
what's wrong with me"*

*"But you said yes when he asked you to marry him
right?"*

"Uh huh"

"So what's the problem then?"

"I don't know"

"Does it have something to do with me?"

"Yes"

"How so?"

*"I don't know....that night at your place changed
everything; but even before that I found myself thinking
about you all the time"*

"Well I do have that effect on women...."

*"Stop kidding around Tom, this really isn't the time...
my whole life is just hanging in the balance and I don't
know what to do and you're making jokes"*

*"I'm sorry, I was just trying to lighten the mood a little;
believe it or not I don't want to see you so unhappy"*

*"That night you saw me in the park I was at your door
earlier just like your neighbor said; I don't know why;
I just found myself there; I just stood there like an idiot*

trying to figure out what to say and try and muster the courage to knock but I noticed Eddy wasn't barking and I started thinking that maybe you moved or something or had been hurt at work or something so I left and then pulled into the park to call Sue to see if she knew anything about where you might be"

"So you do care about me; I knew it; but you know I take Eddy to the park every night for a run"

"I know, I know, but I wasn't thinking clearly; everything is just a blur lately; with work and Mike and his family and everything; I don't know anything anymore...it's all moving so fast and spinning out of control"

"So what are you saying?"

"That's the problem; I don't know what I'm saying; and I don't know what I'm doing anymore"

"That night you and I made love at my place got to you didn't it"

"Yes it did! There I said it!...but it was just another night of sex to you"

"Wow, you really are screwed up fancy pants; in case you haven't noticed I've been crazy about you since the moment I laid eyes on you and that evening we had together was just about the best night of my life; so no, it wasn't just another night of sex for me; I don't even date much because all I can fucking think about is you all the time; so there! I said it too!"

"Oh Tom I've made such a mess of this whole thing and I'm so sorry I treated you so badly"

"That doesn't matter now; but I would like to know why; it's my job isn't it"

"I don't know, I guess I just imagined my life being different"

"My job isn't good enough?"

"Your job is fine Tom; you should be proud of what you do for the people of this city; I realize that now"

"There are a lot of people that rely on guys like me; without us this city would literally shut down; but hey, I don't wear a suit so I guess that makes me a loser huh?"

"I feel so stupid for thinking that way and I'm so very sorry Tom; you really are a good man; you work hard and have a home and you've made a nice life for yourself; and I love watching you and Eddy playing together; it's so adorable....I can see how much you love him and how much he loves you"

"So how come we're not together then? Didn't you have a nice time when we made love that night at my place?"

"Yes"

"You mean it actually compared to the maestro?"

"How do you know about the maestro thing?"

"Sue...she tells me about you; and him; I call her every week or we get together and I ask about you; you're always the topic of discussion fancy pants"

"So how come you never told me?"

"Because you didn't want to hear it and you never gave me a chance; all I ever got from you was insults whenever I'd see you and then you'd slag me behind my back to everyone you know...some of that stuff got back to me....so what the hell was I supposed to do...beg?"

"Oh boy, I'm so incredibly stupid"

"You still didn't answer my question"

"About?"

"The night we made love....was it as good as it is with him...I understand he's dated more women than I'll probably ever meet in my entire life so I'm just curious"

"I'm not really comfortable talking about it but Mike certainly does know his way around a woman's body"

"So I guess being with me wasn't much good in comparison then"

"Well Mr. Sewer guy; I hate to say it but it was better with you...I felt things I'd never felt before when we made love; I can't even describe it; it just felt so right in my heart and soul; I've never felt that with Mike...or anyone...ever...so there...happy?"

"No, because you obviously love this guy despite what you say"

"I do love him; I think; but maybe that love is more friendship than anything else; we have a lot of fun together and he really is a nice guy but that night with you was...God, I don't know; different than anything I had ever felt before; it was really and truly magical and I'll never forget it as long as I live Tom; but it also frightened me; I didn't know what to do so I just ran and hid and lashed out at you as if you had done something wrong"

"Sue told me about your childhood and your dad and all that stuff"

"Oh shit; like I'm not embarrassed enough already?"

"Geezuz Christ fancy pants can't you see a connection here?"

"A connection with what?"

"Oh come on, Eve, your dad!"

"Oh him"

"Yeah, him! Has it ever occurred to you that your obsession with these idiotic suit and tie guys and all that bullshit has something to do with your blue collar dad and all the bad stuff associated with him and the stuff that went on with your mom and all that?"

"Sure, I guess"

"Eve, you don't even see it; you think every guy that doesn't wear a suit or that reminds you of your old man is going to screw your life up and leave you... you equate me with him even though we're completely different people"

Eve sat quietly for a moment and sipped her third double Manhattan as she stared into space.

"Is there something wrong with not wanting bad history to repeat itself?"

"Not at all; but fuck, you've made a goddamn career out of it! You can't go around assuming that every guy that works construction or drives a truck is a shitty person and their only goal in life is to treat you like crap and then leave you....that's fuckin ridiculous!....most of us blue collar guys are good honest hardworking guys with families and children...and yeah sure, we don't have the ivy league educations that some of those professional guys have but we're damn good at our jobs and it doesn't mean we're stupid!"

"You're right; fuck; I've really made a mess of my life; at least the personal part; at least the work part is still good"

"Well that's just great then! But Eve, there's more to life than just wanting a big fancy position with some company that doesn't give a shit about its employees or anything but their precious frikin bottom line"

"The company I work for cares about me and all of us"

"Really!...when your ideas dry up one day and you stop being the wondergirl of the advertising world they'll drop your ass so fast your head will spin...but that doesn't matter...it's work; I'm talking about you...your inability to see what's right in front of you because of some stupid fucking notion you've been carrying around in your head since you were a kid; and hey, I get it; your old man and your mom fucked up pretty bad and you suffered real bad for it; I understand that but Geezuz, get over it for fuck sakes and resolve this thing! Marrying Mike, who I'm sure despite all my kidding and shit is a nice guy underneath all that fancy armor he wears....is not the man for you; he's got money and power and he can basically do anything he wants to do...he may love you now but what happens in three years or ten years when he gets bored and his eye starts to wander...what then....he has a reputation for a reason; you need to keep that in mind or you're going to get hurt...I guarantee it!"

"He would never do that to me"

"Maybe, maybe not....the point is I can't predict that any better than you can; All you can do is look at someone's past track record to see where they're headed and yeah, no guarantees you'll be right. But look, I'm not trying to talk you out of marrying him; I just want to make sure you'll be happy with whatever you choose to do so you can live with yourself....I know you don't really care about money or any of that shit; you're from the country like me; we weren't raised like that; sure money is good because it puts food on the table and buys you

a night out at Denny's now and then but Christ, there's more to life"

"Denny's?"

"Please princess don't act like you don't know what Denny's is or that you haven't eaten there; you probably love eating there; it's me, Tom, you can drop all the bullshit; and hey, what about kids? Let me guess, his highness really doesn't want any right?"

"Sue told you didn't she"

"She didn't have to; I can tell by just looking at the guy; he just wants to have fun; vacations, the office, more vacations, fancy cars, more vacations, the club, his pals....a carefree life; he doesn't want the responsibility of caring for a child; just fun time all the time; can you see him pushing a stroller while you guys take a walk with your dog in the park...c'mon! Those are the special moments in life; not some fucking vacation in the south of France or getting a new Mercedes for your birthday; that's bullshit; and if that's the kind of life you want then that's fine; but it's not the kind of life I want!"

"So you're saying you'd like to have kids?"

"Ya got that right! At least two or three; and I'll tell ya something else; I'm going to be a great dad"

"I believe you Tom; you would be an amazing dad!"

"Damn straight I would! What kind of life is it without kids?....no point in getting married at all as far as I'm concerned if there's no kids...it's not a family"

At this point Eve was starting to not only see reality for the first time but she was starting to gain a little insight into her own problems and her behavior.

She was also starting to get extremely drunk from the Manhattans she had been guzzling down one after the other like water and curled up on the sofa and pulled a throw blanket over her feet;

"Oh my!"

"What's wrong?"

"I'm really really getting drunk all of a sudden"

Tom gently took the glass from her hand;

"Well I think maybe you've had enough of this stuff for one night fancy pants"

*"Tommy.... (*Now slurring her words as the full effect of the alcohol took effect) *I really love your dog...he's so cute....so soft...I could just snuggle up next to him (*as her speech slowed) *safe and sound and sleep...I love you Tommy"*

At that point Eve drifted off into a deep intoxicated sleep. Tom picked her up and carried her to bed and tucked her in still dressed and just stood there at the foot of the bed for a few moments watching her in her slumber and then spoke to her knowing full well she would not hear or remember any of it.

"Well fancy pants I guess this is goodbye; I know you're gonna marry Mike no matter what I say to you so you

probably won't see me again; have a good life...I'll always love you Eve"

Tom turned around and walked out of the room and out of Eve's life.

Chapter 16

The next day Eve didn't go into work. She was horribly hung over from the Manhattan's the night before and she had discovered a note Tom left for her which read;

Dear fancy pants; don't worry, nothing happened last night; you passed out and I put you to bed and then I left. It's too bad we didn't have a chance to really talk and get to know each other sooner but I guess fate has its own plan so all I can do is say that I wish you and Mike a good life together. There's nothing I can say to keep you from marrying him; and who can blame you; I guess most girls would jump at the chance for the kind of life he can give; I can't offer you anything like that so I'm going to get out of your hair now and you probably won't see me again. I'm glad you finally found your perfect fit.

Love always,

Tom

Although she felt wonderful about Tom revealing his feelings towards her she was now more conflicted than ever so she decided to call Gail and tell her she'd be away from work and out of town for at least a week as a personal emergency came up and to reschedule her meetings and so forth.

She also called Mike and told him the same thing. She lied; again.

But she had to; otherwise he'd want to come and see her so she made up a story about having to go back home to see her mom because she was sick. In reality she just wanted the world to stop and everything and everybody to just go away for a while so she could think about things and perhaps start to sort out the tangled mess her life had become.

She suddenly realized that she had a lot of growing up to do and also that she had some emotional baggage that needed to be sorted out and that meant some serious alone time…with the exception of seeing Sue and Lena ….she needed their support more than ever.

For the first three days all she did was wander around her apartment and think about Mike; then about Tom; back and forth. She thought about the wonderful times she had had with Mike and also about the conversation she had with Tom and that night at his place in Queens and Eddy and having kids.

Then she thought about what Tom had said about her issues regarding her father and the effect it had had upon her life and her expectations regarding a mate. She thought about it frontwards and backwards and every which way until she couldn't think about it anymore.

On the fourth day of solitude during a walk in Central Park everything suddenly made sense and she knew exactly what she needed to do. Accordingly she texted Lena and Sue and requested their presence at her apartment for dinner and drinks the next night.

They of course knew that something was going on and that Eve had not left town and were sworn to secrecy particularly where Mike was concerned. But she hadn't explained the real reasons for her vanishing act; just that she needed some time to sort some things out and the girls were to let-on that Eve had left town to attend to her sick mother if asked by anyone.

Thursday evening arrived quickly.

"Well finally, she surfaces"

"Hi girls, come on in" Eve said as she welcomed Sue and Lena at her suite door.

They both barged in like they were crossing the finish line of the New York City Marathon eager to open the bottle of wine they brought along and hear all about the reasons for all the cloak and dagger secrecy and seclusion.

"Ok young lady, this better be good ; you've been cooped up in this apartment all week doing god knows what....are you ok?"

"I am now! Ummm... where to start; let's see; okay; Tom was here several nights ago...I'm surprised he didn't say anything to you Sue"

"To be perfectly honest I haven't talked to him yet this week...oh my god....tell me you didn't..."

"No we didn't....we just talked"

"About?"

"About a lot of things but let me start at the beginning because there are a few things you guys need to know"

"Oh shit...this sounds really serious"

"Ok....so remember when I had lunch with Sessile a while back and told her that everything was fine with Mike's parents and all that stuff? Well I don't know what happened but that night I found myself at Tom's door for some strange reason. He wasn't home but I saw him at the park with Eddy"

"Oh my God....you guys did it in the park"

"I knew you'd say that; but no we didn't do it in the park or anywhere else so just forget about that stuff for now; anyway, he didn't see me until I was leaving after just sitting there watching him and Eddy run around on the grass for about a half hour or so. As I sat there watching them I suddenly realized that my life is completely screwed up"

"So what does that mean exactly?" Lena inquired sensing that Eve had finally started to make some progress in resolving her issues.

"I started to realize what a great guy Tom really is...you should have seen him playing with Eddy; they were so free; it was just one of those rare truly genuine moments that make you question yourself and everything you've been doing with your life; I can't remember the last time I've had a special moment like that with a pet or person that I love; you could just see it in his eyes....it made me cry"

"And then you did it?"

"No, and stop that already! Anyway, as I was driving away Tom saw me and we looked at each other for a brief moment; he saw me watching him and signaled for me to stop and come to him and started running towards my car but I just drove away; and then about a week ago he showed up here out of the blue wanting to talk; so we mixed some drinks and really talked things out"

"Things like?"

"Me and Mike and my dad and my mom and all the crap I've been carrying around since I was a little girl"

Both Lena and Susan's eyes welled up.

"So what did you discover?"

"That I'm a fucking idiot, that's what! I guess I sort of realized it all along but I didn't if you know what I

mean; but I've been basically missing the trees for the forest; I've probably cheated myself out of love time and time again because of the ridiculous standards I've been setting for my perfect fit guy; all that nonsense about professional guys being good and anyone that works in a uniform or jeans and t-shirts being bad; all because I would equate that with my dad and things that happened when I was young that weren't even his fault; god, he tried his best with my mom but she was a mess way before he ever even thought about leaving; I've completely forgotten or repressed all memories of my mother's adultery and the alcoholism that started soon after I was born; I had it all backwards; not that I even want to blame anyone; things just went sideways and never recovered and I ended up in the middle"

"But you rose to the occasion beautifully Eve... look at what you've accomplished in life; you have a wonderful apartment, a great job that pays well and you're respected by your peers at work and certainly by us your friends; and you are about to marry the man of your dreams and have a fairytale wedding and a beautiful life"

"But I want kids!"

"What?"

"I want kids! I want a real family; husband and children and a dog and cat and a nice little home with a yard; I don't want to live in some stuffy mausoleum high above Park Avenue; I want to watch my husband work out in the yard in the summer and bring him lemonade and make him lunch and kiss him at the door when he goes

to work in the mornings and tell him how much I love him and make beautiful babies and raise them and grow old together and see the kids get married and have children of their own...my god, I don't even know what the hell I'm doing here...this is not me....this is not at all who I am....sure I love the clothes and the lunches but it's all just window dressing and at the end of the day is completely meaningless; I've been living a lie all this time and I have to fix it....I have to fix me"

Eve went into the kitchen to check on dinner and came out moments later with two more bottles of wine.

"That's fantastic Eve; but ummm.....you're supposed to be getting married soon to Mike....you fought so hard to gain acceptance from his family so what are you saying? You don't want to marry him now?"

"Exactly!"

"But what are you going to tell him?"

"The truth!"

"Which is?"

"Which is that I do love him but the kind of life he lives is just not for me; I don't belong here and although I'll always love Mike and consider him my best friend after you two of course, I can't live a lie....and he doesn't want kids....I didn't think I did either but I was just fooling myself and got caught up in wanting everything to be so perfect I overlooked every single thing that was important to me; I was just fooling myself to fit in and

try and be what he wanted me to be....but I can't do that anymore; I won't; it's so wrong!"

"So what happens now?"

"Well, several things; first, I'm going to go to work tomorrow and hand in my resignation and talk to Mike while I'm there and tell him that I can't marry him; then I'm going to call a realtor and put this apartment on the market; then I'm going to go back home and straighten out my goddamn stupid screwed up life"

"So this straightening out your life thing back home... what exactly does that entail?"

"I'm going to buy a cute little house with a white picket fence and a yard and start thinking about what I'd really like to do with my life; then I'm going to get my mom into rehab and make sure she gets better and actually be around to make sure she recovers and starts to live a real life clean and sober; and then I'm going to call my father and we are going to sit down and talk things out and we are going to have a proper father daughter relationship the way it should be"

"Oh my god, Eve, that's so amazing and I'm so happy for you; I was starting to think you'd never come around and see the light...I know you've been struggling with these issues for years and both Sue and I have wanted so desperately to see you confront and deal with this stuff but you always seem to pull away at the last second and nothing ever seemed to get resolved...until Tom came along"

"Why didn't you say anything Lena?"

"Because a situation like this requires the person to take the journey and discover these revelations on their own; I could have filled your head with psychobabble ten hours a day but it wouldn't have sunk in; friend or therapist; it didn't matter; you wouldn't have listened... or rather heard what Sue or I were trying to tell you"

"I suppose you're right...I don't know how he did it but Tom got through to me somehow; if it wasn't for the talk we had last week I don't think I would have actually come to terms with any of this"

"That's interesting Eve; by going to him you, although not fully recognizant of it, were asking for help from a man that you felt safe with physically and emotionally; that's the quality and comfort you have always been talking about wanting in a man...and that my dear constitutes a perfect fit in my book! Evie, you are in love with Tom and we all know he's in love with you"

"Well doc I think you've hit the nail on the head... seriously Lena, I really hadn't thought about any of this in quite those terms...and yes for some reason I did feel safe with Tom, I think I told you guys about that (the girls nod) *but yeah, he infuriates me and at the same time I feel good around him...it's the strangest thing ever!"*

"Yeah, strange doesn't even begin to describe any of this but I'm just glad you've decided what to do and to be with Tom"

"Hold on there sister; who said anything about being with Tom?"

"Of course you don't want to be with Tom; that would have made perfect sense and I can see we're just not going in that direction with any of this" Sue said jokingly.

"Well ladies I'm talking about spending some time with me and getting to know me better before I consider inflicting myself and my issues upon anyone else"

"So what are you going to tell Tom?"

"I'm not telling him anything; he left me this goodbye note (Eve hands it over to sue and Lena to read) *so I gather he's had enough of my shenanigans and has decided to move on with his life...I think that's pretty clear judging from what he says there"*

"I hate to be a stickler but as your attorney I must point out that contents of this letter or rather note, is based on the premise that you would be going through with your marriage to Mike...which you are obviously not"

Eve read the note again;

"You know I hate it when you're right dontcha councilor...."

"Yes, I'm aware of that but the big question is what the heck are you going to do about it?"

"What, you being right? I think I can live with that now and then as long as it doesn't become a habit"

"Not that, the other thing"

"What other thing?"

"TOM for Christ sake!"

"Oh that!....ummm....let's see...mmmm....I'm going to do nothing!...the note and whatever it is or isn't based upon changes nothing; yes I'd love to be with Tom and if it's meant to be then it'll work out in the end...but right now I need space"

"Well that's a silly line of reasoning if I ever heard one! You've got a fantastic guy who wants to be with you forever and have babies with you and you just walk away?" Susan said still in 'legal eagle' mode and obviously disappointed that Tom and Eve wouldn't be getting together at least for the moment and possibly never if she didn't take action.

"Actually it's not as silly as you might think Sue; speaking for a moment as a psychotherapist I'd have to agree with Evie; the only thing she needs right now is to work on herself; everything comes second...I mean you and I have been waiting so long for her to get to this point and now that's it's here you can't deny her what she needs the most which is time; time to be alone and get away from this godforsaken city and get in touch with herself and her family and then when she's ready she can start thinking about a relationship again...it could take a week a month a year or ten years; no one can say for certain but ultimately she needs to come to terms in her own way and I'm confident she'll do just that and we both need to support that decision!"

"So what do we say to Tom when he asks why you've suddenly vanished and moved back to Indiana?"

"You tell him whatever you like as long as you include the fact that for the foreseeable future I need space and am not interested in a relationship with anyone so he needs to get on with his life and just forget about me and under no circumstances is he to waste his time waiting for me to suddenly be ok and come back; I honestly don't have a clue how long it will take for me to get my shit together; it may never happen and I'm not going to drag him along for the ride"

"You know damn well he'll come after you wherever you go"

"His job is here in New York; he can't just pick up stakes and come running after some crazy chick living in shitsville Indiana population 500....geez, the poor guy looks like he's just scraping by financially and he wouldn't even be able to afford the airfare to come and see me....and he can't come see me if he doesn't know where I live can he! And that means neither of you better tell him my mom's address; and when I buy a house you better not give that address either"

"Alright, if that's what you want then we'll respect your wishes sweetie"

"Thank you!"

"So when do you plan on leaving?"

"Two days...so if there's anything in the apartment you guys want, including my furniture, clothes and shoes and bags just help yourself...I'll leave you each a key and you can come and take whatever you like"

"What are you going to use for money until your apartment is sold....we can loan you money if you need it"

"I really appreciate that but I've got enough money saved and invested to buy a house back home....they're super cheap there...it's in the middle of nowhere for god sake.... no one wants to live out there...and the real estate agent can handle the sale of the apartment in the meantime; we can fax whatever we need to so there is no reason for me to hang around but I would appreciate it if you handle the sale and paperwork and so forth for me Sue"

"Consider it done; just give me your realtors card and we'll take care of it...I'll have an authorization form sent to you tomorrow that allows me to handle all aspects of the sale on your behalf; sign it and send it over to my office and we're good to go"

Lena cut in; *"So are you going to come back Eve or is this goodbye?"*

They all started crying and hugging.

"Of course we will stay in touch; we have phones and we can fly back and forth to see each other; and as soon as I get settled I want you to come and stay with me for a couple of weeks....agreed?"

"Agreed!"

"Now ladies, lets enjoy our evening and look toward the future"

"Cheers!"

They raised their glasses for a toast.

Chapter 17

Friday morning came quickly but not because it was a hard night of drinking into the wee hours. The girls had left Eve's by eleven at which time Eve turned in and had a particularly long and peaceful night's sleep for the first time in ages.

Mike was under the assumption that Eve wouldn't be back in town until Sunday night which she thought would work in her favor; the element of surprise. Not that she had any malicious intent; quite the contrary as she simply didn't want to create any more drama than necessary; simply go to the office, speak to Mike and then deliver her resignation to Mr. Ballantine and get out of there.

Unlike any other day she had gone to the office this time Eve didn't muss and fuss with her wardrobe; she put on minimal makeup, brushed out her hair and put it in a ponytail to help beat the summer heat, slipped into a pair of jeans, a simple top, put on her lucky socks and sneakers, grabbed her bag and off she went at about 10 a.m.

She hailed a cab and headed straight for the office; first stop Mike. She tried to remain strong and went over what she would say to him over and over in the cab. The last thing she wanted to do was hurt him but there was really no way to avoid it; no matter how she delivered the news it would be extremely painful for him and she deeply regretted that but she had to do what she believed was right in her heart.

She also thought about how disappointed Mike's mom and family would be and felt genuinely bad for any time Betsy had spent in the preliminary stages of planning the wedding but there was nothing she could do; it had to be this way.

There she was; standing on the sidewalk in front of the building that she had worked in for the last six years or so for the very last time. She briefly thought about how far she had come and was happy with what she had accomplished professionally...overall it had been a wonderful and positive experience.

She took a deep breath and went in. When she got out of the elevator she marched straight to Mike's office and spoke with his secretary;

"Hi Marcy, I really need to speak with Mike, is he in?"

"Welcome back Eve, we're all sorry to hear your mom has been having difficulties...but yes, Mike is here

somewhere but I'm not sure where he is at this precise moment...shall I call him for you?"

"No don't bother; if you see him tell him I need to speak with him at some point today...I'm going to leave a note for him on his desk and then I have to run"

"As you wish Eve....nice to see you"

"Thank you Marcy, likewise"

Eve trotted down the hall; it was the first time she didn't click and clack during that walk on the marble floor tiles not to mention the first time her feet weren't hurting at work.

She tried Mike's office door but it was locked; she hadn't a lot of time to waste so she just let herself in with her key...only to find Mike seated on the guest sofa with a young female intern on his lap, her clothing in a slight state of disarray; skirt pulled up and blouse open.

Mike jumped up like he had just received an electric shock dumping the leggy young intern to the floor.

"Eve, I didn't expect you back until Sunday"

"Obviously not!"

"This isn't what it looks like!"

"Of course it isn't Maestro!"

Eve turned and walked out of Mikes office like a woman on a mission; no tears, no muss; no fuss and headed straight for Ballantine's office to hand in her resignation.

He was in a meeting and wouldn't be available for an hour or so but she had no intention of spending a minute more in that building than was absolutely necessary. She handed the envelope that contained her resignation letter to his secretary and walked out of that building for the last time.

Next stop; lunch with Sessile.

"Your message sounded urgent Eve, is everything alright; weren't you supposed to be away until Sunday?... and I love what you're wearing by the way; it looks super comfortable"

"It is; the sneakers are so comfy; I never went anywhere"

"Pardon? I don't understand"

"The last week, I was home; I can't marry Mike"

"Oh no, what happened?"

"I've spent the entire week alone thinking about things; my life is a mess Sessile and I have to fix it"

"A mess? Any girl would love to trade their life for your mess; you're about to marry into one of the most powerful families in the country...you will have everything you ever dreamed of"

"Yeah, sure; everything but the one thing I've been looking for all my life"

"What's that?"

"A perfect fit!"

"What do you mean sweetie, I'm sorry ...I'm not following you"

"You know...a life that fits; like a great pair of shoes; comfort, style, substance...always there when you need them to make you feel good; you know...like these sneakers"

"Ok" Sessile said cautiously thinking for a moment that perhaps Eve had lost her mind or had developed a case of heat stroke or something.

"Sess; a life with Mike and his family is not a perfect fit for me; I'm a country girl; that's where I belong; I quit my job this morning and am headed back home to Indiana the day after tomorrow"

"Oh my god....Mike is going to be totally crushed; have you thought about what this will do to him; he loves you so much and this is going to absolutely kill him; have you even considered his feelings in all this self-discovery of yours? I must say I'm a little disappointed...I mean I understand...sort of... but I don't understand if you know what I mean...I'm confused I guess is what I'm saying ...have you told him yet?....oh my god he's going to need Sebastian's support more than ever...how could you do this to him.....to all of us...we welcomed you into the family....and we..."

Eve cut her off;

"I went to see Mike an hour ago"

"Poor Michael....I feel so bad...how did he take it?"

"I don't know Sessile"

"What do you mean?"

"He was busy playing touchy feely with an intern on his lap so I never got the chance to say anything"

"Oh god! I'm so sorry Eve; What an idiot! Did he say anything?"

"Oh yes, that he didn't expect me back until Sunday"

"Wow, that's it? No explanations or anything?"

"I just walked out; I wasn't interested in hearing any of his bullshit!"

"Maybe there's a way to fix this"

"Sessile; I just caught him with another woman on his lap; how do you come back from that; pretty self-explanatory don't you think? I mean what could he possibly say to fix something like that? Please!"

Sessile just sat there dumfounded; but on some level not surprised at all; she knew it would be a matter of time before he reverted back to his womanizing; much like her own relationship with Sebastian.

"I'm so sorry Eve...and here I am giving you shit for breaking his heart; I'm an idiot! I was hoping that Mike and Sebastian would grow out of this nonsense by now but I must say you appear to be handling it extremely well"

"Ever think about leaving Sebastian?"

"Christ I wish I had the guts; but I'm not as strong as you are and to be perfectly honest I don't really care what he does; it sounds horrible; I just look the other way and don't ask questions; and if I happen to meet someone that interests me here and there I may indulge in a little extracurricular activity myself...I guess that's part of my own perfect fit as you put it"

"Well, I'm certainly not one to judge others given the way I've screwed up my life; you've been a good friend throughout all this Sess and I'm just sorry things didn't work out; I've enjoyed your company and am really glad we met; I sincerely mean that"

"Thank you Eve; same here; I want you to have the kind of life that you want; you've got guts girl; I'll always admire you for that!"

After their final luncheon Eve headed back to her apartment to find Mike sitting on the floor outside her suite door.

"How did you get in here?"

"I slipped in with a delivery guy"

"So what do you want?"

"I want you Eve!"

"I'm sorry; did you sustain a head injury on the way over here? I just walked in on you with one of the interns on your lap not four hours ago you stupid idiot so you can take those flowers you're holding and stick em straight up your ass pal!"

"I wasn't going to sleep with her; I just..."

"Just what Maestro?...just got caught before you could get her panties off and finish your important little meeting?"

"That was the first time; I swear! Nothing happened!"

"Nothing happened? Geezuz Mike, please! Stop the fucking bullshit! You were in your locked office playing kissy kissy with another woman! I don't think you're even capable of distinguishing between the truth and lies anymore. And you have the nerve to come here and tell me that it was nothing? Go tell her it was just nothing and see what she says! You'll never change and I should have recognized that from the start and steered clear of you altogether; you and your fancy apartment and all that sincere talk about not bringing any other girls up there and all your fancy cars and the Hampton's; it's all utterly pathetic; you're an idiot and I don't ever want to see you again; go marry Abby and keep up the status quo of lies and deception so your family can be proud; what a bunch of sad and empty people you all are; there's no amount of money in the world that can change that!"

"I'm so sorry Eve; we can fix this; I love you!"

"Oh shut up! You haven't a clue what love is! Grow up; you're just a spoiled overindulged child in a man's body! But it really doesn't matter anyway because I was on my way over to your office to tell you that I can't marry you and that I've quite my job and am leaving town the day after tomorrow"

*"For a vacation? Hey maybe we can go together....
my brother has a villa in Spain that we could use for a
couple of weeks and just sort this mess out"*

*"You're not hearing me Mike; I'm leaving for good; I'm
going back home and starting over again"*

*"Eve, I promise, this little oversight will never happen
again"*

*"You're still not hearing me Mike; it's not about you and
your inability to keep your dick in your pants; it's about
me reassessing my life....it's not always about you and
your family and what you people want; I'm doing what's
right for me for the first time"*

*"So what can I do....I'll do anything Eve ...please!....
don't go!"*

*"I think you're more worried about word getting around
that you've been dumped than anything else"*

*"I don't care about that...we have to work this out; what
am I going to tell my mom?"*

*"That you're an idiot and you screwed up the one
chance of real happiness that you will ever have for
a dirty little titty feel and dry hump in your office; I'd
start with that!"*

*"I refuse to let you go; let's go inside and talk this
out and everything will be fine; you're just upset right
now"*

"I'm not upset Mike; I'm just done! I'm going inside now and you're leaving" Eve said as she unlocked her door and stepped inside.

As she tried to close the door Mike said *"I'm coming in and we're going to talk about this whether you like it or not"*

"What are you five years old?...I said go away Mike, I mean it"

Mike shoved the door open and grabbed Eve by the arm but she refused to be bullied as she looked him in the eye and said;

"Really? So what are you going to do beat me up now because you didn't get your way? Wow, what a big man; your parents must be so proud!"

"You're not going to do this to me Eve; I won't allow it!"

"HEY! The lady wants you to leave buddy; I think you better listen to her"

Tom suddenly materialized from down the corridor.

"Tom, what are you doing here?" Eve said; secretly relieved to see him.

"I got a call from Sue; she was worried about you. I figured this piece of shit might be around to bother you today so I took the afternoon off to keep an eye on things"

Mike spoke up; *"This doesn't concern you Tom so go crawl back into your sewer like a good boy"*

Tom chuckled and shook his head; walked over to Mike, grabbed him by the scruff of his suit jacket and yanked him out of Eve's doorway like a rag doll throwing him to the floor of the hallway and said;

"I have a better idea bud, why don't you leave before you get hurt"

"Do you think I'm scared of you?"

"I'd have to say yes to that one Nancy; I kind of got that impression; so what's it gonna be pal; you can walk out of here or go out on a stretcher; your choice!"

Mike scrambled to his feet and punched Tom in the face; he saw it coming but didn't think there was any particular need to move out of the way.

Tom just shook his head and said *"So that's it? That's all you got? Geezuz, dude you punch like a little girl"* and hit Mike with a lighting fast punch that knocked him out cold.

When he came-too a few moments later tom said *"so you still wanna fight or are you ready to leave now; don't make me lose my temper; now do yourself a favor and just walk away"*

Tom helped Mike to his feet and escorted him out of the building and said *"If I ever hear that you've gone anywhere near Eve again I'll come looking for you; got that?"*

Mike just stumbled off mumbling to himself and yelling *"This isn't over, I'll get you for this...I know some very powerful people"*

Tom just replied *"Alrighty Nancy nice to see you too; let's play golf on the weekend; my best to the family! Drive safe now!"* smiling and waving to Mike as he staggered off to his Mercedes parked just down the block.

Tom buzzed Eve to get back into the building and went up to make sure she was ok.

She handed him a cold beer as he walked in with his big construction boots;

"I had that situation well in hand Tom; I didn't need you to do that; you could have really hurt him!"

"Ya got that right!"

"Ok Mr. tough guy; I guess I owe you a thank you for coming to my rescue; not that I needed it; I was just about to kick his ass when you showed up"

"I don't doubt it Eve but to be honest I've been wanting to do that for a longtime and well, I guess today was the day"

"So what did Sue tell you?"

"Not much; all I could get out of her was that you have decided not to marry Richie Rich and need some time to sort some things out"

"yeah...look Tom...I know there is something special going on between us but I'm such a mess right now I just need to be alone for a while and sort things out...it would be a mistake to start something that I might not be capable of finishing"

"So where does that leave us?"

"I don't know, I need time"

"Ok...if that's what you want then I guess you'll just have to follow your heart; I was going to leave you alone like I said in my note but when I heard you were headed to the office to dump buttercup I figured he might come sniffing around to cause trouble so I sat across the street at the café and waited for him to show up"

"Oh Tom, you really are a wonderful guy and I know now that you genuinely do care for me and part of me just wants to jump into your arms right now and go off to your house and never leave"

"So why don't you? I know it's a small house and it's not fancy enough for ya but we could get a bigger house; I want to take care of you and protect you...you me and Eddy could have a nice life together fancy pants!"

"I have issues out the ying yang with my mom and my dad and all kinds of things...I need to deal with that... please try and understand"

"Actually, last week when we talked and you drank yourself silly you told me you loved me right before you passed out; do you remember that?"

"Oh my god I'm so embarrassed!"

"Don't be; I know I kid you a lot and we've have our share of arguments and battles but just for the record; you'll always be special to me; I just wanted to let you know that; but you're not ready for any of this and to be honest I don't want to be in a one sided relationship so I'm going to go now...you take care fancy pants!"

Tom walked out of her life...again.

After a good cry in the kitchen as Eve sorted through her things she decided to call the girls over for one last dinner in that apartment together on the Saturday night.

They had a wonderful time together talking about all sorts of things and of course Eve relayed the events of the previous day with Mike and his infidelity, her lunch with Sessile, the incident with Mike in the hallway at her place and how Tom came to her rescue and beat Mike to a pulp and sent him on his way.

She also asked if either of the girls had told Tom that she was leaving town to go back home and start over. As per her instructions they hadn't; and neither did she during her talk with him the previous day and she wanted to keep it that way and made them promise to not say anything about her whereabouts.

The next day she got on a plane alone with nothing but a carry-on bag and flew away.

Chapter 18

When Eve arrived home in Indiana she stayed with her mother for a couple of months during which time she somehow convinced her to seek help for her drinking problem.

As anticipated she was quite resistant at first but Eve was relentless and finally her mom gave in. That marked the pivotal first step in new life for both Eve and her mom.

In the months that followed, Eve bought a beautiful little house just down the street from her mom's place so she'd be close by to make sure she stayed off the bottle. Having Eve there made all the difference in the world; she desperately wanted to get better; partially for herself and mostly for Evie's sake to try and make up for all the pain she had caused; she was genuinely grateful to have been given the opportunity and a second chance at being the kind of mom that Eve could be proud of.

They became friends for the first time and would walk over to each other's house each day and sit out on the porch sipping coffee, smoking cigarettes and just talking about whatever came up while her mom's dog and faithful companion of eight years Ophelia lay there at their feet while the branches of the big willow trees in the yard swayed back and forth in the warm breeze under the crystal blue sky.

Of course Eve relayed the details of her brief romance with Mike and told her all about the wonderful guy named Tom that she met as well but had to leave behind. At first her mom didn't understand any of it…and who would? It was all such a mess.

Her mom couldn't believe that anyone would walk away from a high paying job in New York City let alone someone like Mike and all that money for a quiet boring life in a small town.

But the more Eve explained the situation and the more they talked about it the more her mom began to understand that it didn't matter what she thought; it mattered what Eve thought and what Eve wanted her life to be. She wanted her little girl to be happy and vowed to do whatever was necessary to help her achieve that.

Eve had also mustered up the courage to call her father and even flew to California to visit him at his home a couple of times in the months that followed. He was still driving a big rig for a living and still remained unattached and appeared quite happy that way; his life was out on the road in his truck and that's where he longed to be.

Things were finally coming together for Eve; she had confronted her demons and felt good about herself for the first time in her life. Yes, of course she longed for Tom and was tempted to call him several times but decided against it; it would be ridiculous to assume that he'd just give up everything and come running thousands of miles to rush to her side to live in some small town.

Part of her wished he would just pop up out of nowhere unexpectedly like he always did and she would often look for him out of the corner of her eye whenever she walked down main street while looking at shop windows or getting groceries; but he didn't come.

She had been talking to Sue via the phone or email since the day she left New York and always inquired about Tom but Sue didn't have much information for her; the basis for Sue's relationship with Tom was mainly based upon Eve so with her gone they didn't have much to say to each other and had according to Sue, lost touch for the most part except for the occasional quick chat if they happened to run into each other.

By the time the next summer rolled around Eve finally came to the realization that she was complete in and of herself; she didn't need a man to define her or complete her and accordingly she finally let Tom go.

Although she had a sizeable chunk of money in the bank from the sale of her Manhattan apartment she started to think about work; not that she had to at the moment and not that she was bored but she wanted to do something; something important; something that really mattered to her and that she would really enjoy and perhaps others could benefit from.

She approached the principal of the local high school with resume in hand and managed to land herself a job teaching an advertising and marketing class three days a week; it didn't pay much at all; just enough to buy groceries and keep gas in her tank and that was good enough for her.

Every Friday afternoon she would go to the local diner and sit in a booth grading papers and chat with the locals, some of whom still remembered her as a gutsy little tomboy and they would recount stories of childhood mischief and reminisce for hours at a time.

Other days Eve would just wander from shop window to shop window enjoying an ice cream cone and the tranquility of small town life; it felt good to finally be home.

She would also visit her neighbor Fiona; a widow of ten years that lived in the big Craftsman style house next door and would go over to help her with her garden and get groceries for her.

They became very close and had many wonderful chats on Fiona's front porch-swing in the late evenings and sometimes Eve's mom would join them and they would barbeque or try cooking new dishes and trade recipes.

Unfortunately a few months later Fiona passed away quietly in her sleep. Eve had lost a good friend and was genuinely saddened but chose to focus on the wonderful times they had shared together.

The town held a big grand ceremony and party in Fiona's honor for being such a good friend to so many of the townsfolk for so many years; she was truly loved by everyone that had the privilege of knowing her.

Her son, a gentleman of about sixty who lived in the neighboring town was in attendance and approached Eve after the ceremony.

"You must be Eve"

"Yes sir"

"I'm Fiona's son Dave; mom told me what a good friend you have been to her and she wanted you to have this envelope"

"Oh my gosh! I don't need anything, really, I have savings and I'm fine; this isn't necessary" she explained assuming it was money.

He chuckled and said *"I don't think its money; she said something about a note"*

"Well that's a relief; thank you so much; your mom was a wonderful person and we enjoyed many a pleasant evening sitting out on the porch swing together and talking for hours; I'll miss her terribly"

"She was very fond of you....anyway, I best get to talkin with the other guests so you'll have to excuse me"

"Of course and thank you so much and my sincere condolences to both you and your wife"

"My wife passed away many years ago but thank you anyway young lady"

Eve took the envelope home and eagerly opened it out on her porch as she sat and sipped cold sweet tea. It was indeed a note written in shaky handwriting that said;

Evie my dear, don't be sad; there is so much joy yet to come; the trick is to know it when you see it, then grab it and have the courage to hold onto it.

Love always, Fiona.

She didn't have the slightest idea what it meant but was just happy that Fiona had taken the time to remember her and leave her with a final thought.

The next day Eve came up with an idea and was upset with herself for not thinking of it sooner during the ceremony while Fiona's son was there; she wanted to buy Fiona's house but with the funeral and all it never dawned on her to ask and besides, it wasn't the right time to discuss such things.

But she didn't fret over it as she assumed that Fiona's son would put the grand old house on the market soon enough and she would have the opportunity to buy it regardless.

Eve loved that old house of Fiona's; it had a grand entry with a huge winding staircase and a big hundred year old chandelier, a parlor, a huge kitchen and original wide plank hardwood floors.

It was in need of some repair work but Eve was convinced that she could fix it up and restore it to its former glory. But it was more than that; the house had a comfort to it; an intangible warmth that tickled her insides whenever she was there; she wanted to feel that sensation every day.

Not that her own house was terrible or anything; it was a lovely little home with a white picket fence just as she had always dreamt of but there was something inexplicably special about Fiona's house.

Eve waited patiently for a couple of weeks but never saw a for sale sign go up so she approached the local real estate agent to inquire but was told that it was not for sale as Fiona's son for whatever reason had not yet decided what to do with it. Eve was of course disappointed but wasn't about to give up that easily.

Every day for a month Eve watched out her kitchen window for signs of life next door at the grand old house but nothing. She had hoped that Dave or someone from Fiona's family would show up so she could talk to them about purchasing the house from them; and she was prepared to offer them quite a handsome price for it.

A few weeks later Eve woke to the sound of voices coming from Fiona's place. Finally she could put her plan into action and attempt to buy the old house she loved so much.

Eve eagerly cut through the bushes that separated the two homes and walked around to the front to discover a delivery truck from the lumberyard and hardware store.

"Hi there!" She said to one of the young men unloading what seemed like the equivalent of an entire forest full of lumber plus endless spools of electrical wire and switches and new windows and so forth; enough materials to completely update and renovate the grand old home.

"Yes maam, can I help you" One of the delivery guys said as he rounded the corner with both hands occupied by several brand new power tools.

She thought to herself; wow I must be getting old or something, that kid just called me maam. But she shrugged it off with a chuckle and asked if the owner was around so she could talk to them.

"No I don't reckon so maam, but I hear they will be here to commence workin on the place by the end of the week"

"Okay then thank you"

Well that was certainly promising news Eve thought to herself; she was certain that once Dave heard her offer he would take it...and she was quite prepared to offer additional money for all the materials that he had apparently paid for.

She didn't know what all those materials were for exactly but was convinced that once Dave explained it to her she could hire a handyman to do the technical work and she would do the painting and decorating and so forth.

That week seemed to go on forever; day by day, minute by minute. Saturday morning she awoke to the sounds of hammering and power tools buzzing next door. The moment of truth had indeed arrived!

She bounded out of bed and into her fuzzy slippers; raced into the shower, threw on a sundress and her favorite sneakers, completely bypassed her former extensive makeup application ritual, did a quick hair brushing and headed over to talk to Dave about the house.

She pounded on the front door and even tried the handle but it was locked; but she could hear the deafening whine of power tools buzzing away inside so she ran back over to her place and scribbled a note to welcome Dave back to the neighborhood, grabbed a pie she had made the day before just for the occasion and ran back to Fiona's to strategically place the note and the pie on the porch where it would be noticed once Dave came up for air.

In the meantime Eve went and attended to some errands in town.

When she returned she could see that the pie and note were still on the porch undisturbed and the pickup truck that was there earlier was gone.

She wasn't sure what to make of it and decided to just go out into the backyard and water her garden as it had been very hot that week. She lit a smoke and went about her business occasionally looking over at Fiona's in anticipation of Dave's return.

Finally she gave up and figured Dave wouldn't be back until the next day so once again her hopes were dashed.

As she stood there watering her flowers enjoying the country music playing on the radio she kept on her back porch something cold poked her leg; startled she looked down to find an adorable Labrador Retriever wagging its tail uncontrollably; it appears she had made a new friend.

"Hey there boy...what's yer name?" she said as she knelt down to pet and play with him; *"are you lost?... aha, I betcha yer Dave's dog arentcha!"*

She headed toward the bushes to cut through with her playful new friend bouncing along happily around her and approached the back door of Fiona's house which was left wide open; she shouted in;

"Hello?....Dave?....it's Eve your neighbor ...are you there?...I brought your dog back"

There was no reply so she pulled out a pack of cigarettes from her sundress pocket and sat down on the back porch for a smoke figuring Dave would be out momentarily and went over her proposal in her mind as she watched the dog run around the huge yard.

"Those goddamn things are gonna kill ya!"

It took a moment to register and she thought "no, it simply can't be!"

For a moment there it sounded like Tom and she thought she had suddenly lost her mind or something.

She looked around but saw no one. Then all of a sudden the dog came charging back toward the house and ran straight in through the open door leading to the kitchen.

Eve turned to find Tom standing there in his trademark t-shirt, jeans, tool belt and construction boots as usual appearing from out of nowhere totally unexpectedly.

She was speechless as the dog came running back out and started licking her and jumping up onto her again like a long lost friend; which was actually the case; it was Eddy!

Eve started to cry as she hugged and petted him;

"Oh my god, Eddy, I missed you so much...did you miss me too buddy?"

"Probably; he doesn't know any better!!"

Eve was speechless and totally overcome with emotion as tears of joy streamed down her face.

"What no hug fancy pants?"

Eve jumped to her feet and leapt up into his arms and they hugged for several minutes as she cried and he did his level best to pretend that he didn't want to...but a few tears found their way to his cheek despite his best efforts to maintain his macho demeanor and wipe them away as if they were just beads of sweat from the heat.

"Took ya long enough to get here Tom you sonovabitch!"

"Women! Christ! First they tell ya to go away and then when ya show up they give you shit for not being there sooner...too much for a simple country boy to understand"

"What in tarnation are you doing here?"

"I live here...what are you doing here?"

"I live here...well, not here...through the bushes there; next door"

"Wow, what a coincidence...small world huh?

"Did Dave hire you to fix this place up? I don't understand"

"Beer first; talk later"

"Where's the pie I left on the front porch?"

"Shit I didn't see it; I've got the front door blocked off from the inside because I'm doing some rewiring around it; had to tear down the plaster as well so it's a mess; tell ya what; you go around front and grab the pie and I'll go get us a couple of beers"

Eve sprinted around to the front yard with Eddy hot on her heels and returned to the back porch to find Tom sitting there with a woman. Her heart just sank as she wondered if this was all just a bad dream and she would suddenly wake up in her bed in Manhattan or if this was some kind of cruel payback.

"Eve I want you to meet Jan"

"So pleased to meet you!" Eve said as she extended her hand as if to shake the hand of the woman that won Tom's heart. Despite felling like she could die right there she kept a stiff upper lip and said *"So you finally got married huh Tom?"*

"Married? Fuck no! This is my sister; she's going to hang out for a couple of weeks and help around the house until I get settled"

"Oh my gosh I'm so sorry, I just assumed..."

"There ya go assuming things again; same old Eve huh?" Tom said as he laughed.

Eve's spirits were immediately lifted.

"So you're not married?"

"Nope"

Jan cut in immediately recognizing that the two of them had much to discuss; *"Well will ya look at the time; I've got some errands to run before supper; it was really nice to meet you Eve"*

Then she turned to Tom and whispered *"She's still gorgeous; don't screw it up this time!"* then punched him in the arm for good measure before trotting off.

Finally the two settled onto the porch swing and fell into conversation as they dug into the pie and enjoyed their cold beers like two old friends.

"Okay buster; what are you really doing here...this is getting really weird!....but good weird if ya know what I mean"

"Yeah I know; but I told you; I live here"

"No you don't, this is Fiona's son Dave's place"

"No it's not"

"What do you mean?"

"Dave is my dad and Fiona was my grandmother; she left me the house and a thousand acres of land on the back ridge"

"Oh my god! The note; that's what she meant"

"What?"

"She left me a note that your dad gave me at the funeral which you didn't attend by the way saying that everything was going to be ok...how could she know?"

"Well I was here; we had a private viewing at the funeral home just for the immediate family the night before the towns public ceremony and then I had to fly back to New York; I just got back here late last night and I told my old man to not say anything to anyone, especially you"

"Why?"

"Because I figured you'd get all weird about it and assume I came here just for you...as if... and then tell me to move and all the rest of it"

"You're probably right!"

"You still don't remember do you!"

"Remember what?"

"Me!"

"What do you mean?"

"Think back to when you were a kid; there was a little boy that would come over here every weekend and the two of you would run around this big ole house laughing and chasing each other and having the time of your lives and play hide and go seek and all kinds of shit....that little boy was me!"

Eve started to cry again *"Little Tommy Wayne? I didn't even make the connection....why didn't you say something to me sooner?"*

"Because I didn't realize it myself until I made Sue tell me where you had gone...then my grandma called me up and said 'that cute little Evie girl' finally came home and I realized who you were; I knew it was fate; I had to come back to finish what we had started all those years ago and I made her promise not to say anything about me to you...I was hoping she'd still be here when I came home but I guess the good lord had other plans"

"Oh my gosh now I remember! You and your family lived over in the next county and would come to visit

Fiona and your grandpa every Sunday and have a big dinner; afterwards you'd always come over to my mom's house looking for me and we'd run down to the creek and catch frogs and stuff...but then one Sunday you didn't come; I waited and waited and cried all night but I never saw you again... where did you go?"

"We moved away because my old man got a good job offer in Nevada; and then when I got a little older my mom died of Cancer and my older brother was killed in action in Iraq and then I left for new York for that sewer job you loved so much but my dad moved back here a few years ago when he retired; can't take the country out of the boy I guess"

"I can't believe this is happening; so you're here to stay...for good?"

"Ya got that right! Livin in the city sucks; couldn't take it anymore so like it or not you're stuck with me...hey.... wanna go catch frogs down by the creek later?"

Eve's eyes welled up and she said *"Yes...I'll come catch frogs with you Tom O'Neil!"*

"About six-ish then at the exclusive members entrance to the crick by the old willow tree?"

"It's a date!" Eve said as she laughed still dabbing the tears from her eyes.

"Good! Well since you're here you may as well come in and take a look at the place; I've got a lot of work to do and I'm gonna need your help with colors and furniture and painting all that crap; are you in?"

"I'll have to check my schedule but yes I think it's pretty safe to say that I'm in!"

"Alright; let's get a move on; I've still got a lot of work to do today and it ain't gonna git done sittin out here jawin all day with the likes of you"

He took her hand and they went inside;

"Shit, I almost forgot to tell ya there's a couple of people waiting for you in the parlor; go have a look and I'll grab us all some more cold beers...goddamn air conditioner is on the fritz....puttin in a central air system next week...wouldn't want you to get all sweaty or anything when you're over here buggin me and distracting me while I'm trying to get work done...and hey..."

"Yes Tom?"

"I love you fancy pants!"

"I love you too sewer guy...this is the part where you kiss me by the way!"

"What, you think I couldn't figure that out?"

"Geez, I don't know, you're taking long enough"

"Complain complain complain...come here you"

After a few minutes Eve went up front to the parlor.... and found Lena and Sue sitting there;

"We figured it was about time for a visit so we hitched a ride with that sewer guy you hate so much!"

A few months later Eve's dad walked her down the aisle of the quaint little town church in her mom's wedding gown complete with comfy sneakers as Tom waited at the alter in a suit and construction boots with Eddy sitting by his side.

A perfect fit!